February 21, 200_

To Peggy   THIS IS NOT ME!

SERVING GRAVY WITH A SLOTTED SPOON

May your life be filled with humor

FREDA GOWER WARD

Freda Gower Ward

AmErica House
Baltimore

First printing

ISBN: 1-58851-979-1
PUBLISHED BY AMERICA HOUSE BOOK PUBLISHERS
www.publishamerica.com
Baltimore

Printed in the United States of America

To Hal, my husband,
without whom there would be
no joy and humor,
to our children and extended family
who are essential to my life,
and to God from whom all thoughts
and words flow

TABLE OF CONTENTS

INTRODUCTION

Almost all of my life I've written stories, many of which were in the form of letters to family and friends. At still other times, a skit, a play, a monologue, a poem for a birthday or special happening, a spiritual thought for the day or a motivational article was written. On one particular day, I decided to write a book.

My plan was to gather the bits that were previously written, edit them, write a few more and combine them into a book. A disciplined schedule would be developed to write at least one page every day. I was certain this could be done, so there was no concern when April 15 rolled around and almost nothing had been accomplished. Several pages could be written each day for the next few months. If this didn't happen, so what. Only a few more were needed for the book anyway. On December 21, I knew it would be a good idea to defer the book and move the deadline into the next century.

Still, the idea persisted. The book would contain material that was motivational, inspirational, spiritual, filled with insight, depth and humor. It would be compelling and uplifting-- providing joy and laughter to the reader.

Ok, so the book wasn't written that year. But when I did get started, the words wouldn't stop. Five books have now been written with two more in the works. All of them are filled with situations that surround each of us and are enormously funny to me. I can see humor in almost everything--and you can, too, if you'll allow yourself to take the happenings out of context. My surroundings, observations, experiences and reactions are similar to those of most women. Likewise, my husband is similar to most others. You may see yourself in this book and say, "been there, done that."

Writing this book has been a joyful experience. I hope you'll find relaxation and pleasure in reading it and sense the zest I felt while writing it.

May God bless you richly in all of your endeavors--especially as you lighten your mood and add laughter to your days.

HIDING

Hal and I have been married so long that each of us knows what the other is thinking before either one ever has the thought--and we delight in interjecting our opinions onto the thoughts of the other. We can look at each other and either nod or say "yes" or "no" or "I believe you misunderstood what you thought I was thinking because I wasn't thinking the thoughts you seem to think I was. You can see that we anticipate each other. Even when we deviate from the norm with our extra-marital affairs of volunteer work, shopping sprees, computer addictions and cleaning obsessions, we're still usually on the same page--except for the time when I decided to hide under the desk.

You see, I may be working in the office, cleaning the bathroom, on a ladder painting or doing something else that is interesting and absorbing to me, and Hal will be in the kitchen. Suddenly, I hear him calling--with urgency. Despite the fact that I know him well, there's always the possibility that he really needs me this time. Probably the sky is falling and his hands are full--so he needs help. So far, however, the sky hasn't fallen; Hal has simply thought of something he wanted to say to me. Instead of going to where I was, he called for me to go to where he was. Sometimes I don't mind--and sometimes I do. Today I did.

He called several times. Wanting to add some spice to my otherwise predictable life, I chose to ignore him--not that this was the first time I had ever done that--and to let him look for me. Soooo, in my infinite wisdom, I crawled under the desk and pulled the chair up to the desk to hide me.

I could visualize his accepting the fact that I was not going to him so he would look for me. He would walk through our home, calling me. He would be flabbergasted. I'm not the

9

type to disappear. He would look on the balcony, on the landing and keep walking and calling.

Well, I thought this was so funny that I nearly split a seam laughing. Remember my cramped space--and the fact that I had forgotten to visit the bathroom before crawling under the desk. These factors made it difficult to laugh--silently--without an accident.

When Hal did not come looking for me, and I decided to make myself miraculously appear, my legs evidently didn't understand the message my brain was sending because I couldn't quite get them untangled. Bear in mind that my carcass had been folded up under the desk for several minutes. The desk is only 22 inches deep to begin with--and not very wide. In addition, there was the chair to contend with. In the first place, the chair that was blocking my egress was not one with rollers--and it didn't want to be pushed on the carpet. I wasn't in much of a position to negotiate with it, and I certainly didn't want Hal to see me in my compromising position. My legs continued to defy me and refused to unfold themselves. They were, if you'll allow me to say it, stiff.

It occurred to me that Hal had probably eaten dinner, gone out for a walk, met friends and might not be back for two or three hours. Or worse yet, he might have sat down in one of the swivel chairs on the deck and gone to sleep. When he woke, if this were the case, he would go directly to bed and wouldn't be sufficiently coherent to know if I was in bed or not-- or even alive.

I was beginning to feel uncomfortable. Suddenly, the situation that held such magnificent humor a few minutes earlier, no longer did.

My desire at this point was to get out of the present predicament. I didn't care if I had to crawl under the chair-- although that was distinctly not an option. There was, indeed, a chair--but for me to crawl under it was not going to happen.

I felt an overwhelming need to escape from my hiding place before Hal found me.

You've heard that the one who laughs last laughs best. In this case, I was the only one laughing; no one knew I was laughing; and, in fact, at this point I wasn't laughing.

Can you imagine a woman of my age hiding under the desk--playing hide and seek with her husband who doesn't even know she's hiding or that he's supposed to seek?

Can you imagine my distress when I realized that my mind-reading skills had failed, and I learned that Hal was sitting on the deck reading a book and hadn't even missed me?

MY SURE DIET

Almost everyone has a favorite diet. The diet often has no bearing on whether or not it works. The fact is everyone must have a diet to be able to make small talk in polite society. The last time I visited the dentist and heard his admonitions about how to care for my teeth, I, too, developed a diet that really works, and I want to share it.

Diets present an easy way to enter the conversation of an established group. How else would you break in? What would you say at the next luncheon if you didn't have a diet and a reason for ordering--or not ordering--a specific food? You can get a great deal of attention by providing an in-depth discussion and analysis of your diet and why it's the best one available. If God didn't want you to have a diet, she would have created all people equally with a svelte figure, well proportioned, looking like a perfect ten in a bathing suit.

Sara's diet calls for vinegar. On everything. Ok, that's no problem. Vinegar on beets, on greens or even green beans is good. So far, so good, but she can't have wheat--except, if it's in white bread or cereal--and if she wants to eat bread or cereal she has to on Tuesday and Wednesday.

Bill has a diet, too. He takes eleven supplement pills/capsules after every meal. He lives on health foods and has for years. But listen to this. He can't have regular cooking oil; he has to have hot pressed oil--or is it cold pressed?

I don't know what either one is. I didn't ask what the benefits of hot or cold pressed are versus luke-warm pressed--or wrinkled. He thinks his oil with seasoning is the best thing to come down the pike and believes it's also healthier than oil pressed at a different temperature.

Just think how Bill and his wife and Sara and her husband could talk together. Of course, each one has a specific diet that will result in the best possible health--when supplemented with the eleven vitamins/minerals/herbs at each meal.

Sara and Bill's diets aren't for losing weight; they're just for general health. Can you imagine traveling, whether for the day or for several days, with enough supplements to last and keeping all of them straight? It would take quite a bit of time just to sort them out into three (or more) piles for any given day. Imagine a supply for two people for one week! They would need more luggage than we allocate for clothes.

Sara has what might be termed a "mixed marriage," in that all of her food is mixed together in a bowl--and her husband's isn't. It's served on a plate.

Perhaps the most astonishing part of most diets is that there are so many "shalt nots" and exceptions. It seems to me that the exceptions are even greater than the shalt nots.

What I really need, though, is one that will specifically eliminate weight gained from eating chocolate. It needs to be simple, devoid of multiple rules and negatives.

Lest you should be wondering, let me assure you right now that I really do have a diet. I know you'll want to hear about it and you'll be anxious to adopt it as soon as you learn its simplicity and value. My diet is easy--and it works.

Well, it works, depending on what you're trying to accomplish. If you're trying to lose weight, you'll want to pay special attention at this point.

My diet is called "Brush, Floss and Rinse." It's simple and there are no other rules or exceptions. You don't have to concern yourself with fat content, carbohydrates or even sweet treats. You don't need a special oil or vinegar.

The way it works is that you eat all you want. When your stomach hurts, you quit eating. You brush your teeth for two minutes, floss and rinse with mouthwash for one minute. When you're finished with that routine, you can't eat or drink for thirty minutes. Well, who would want to? You're exhausted by that time and need a nap.

When you eat again, regardless of how tiny and insignificant the food item is, you must repeat the brush, floss and rinse regimen. Following that routine three times each day is about all I can handle. If I snack between meals, I have to --well, you know the requirement by now--and it just isn't worth it. It doesn't make any difference what the food temptation is, it just isn't worth it--if you have to brush, floss and rinse.

Now, you remember Sara and her diet. Well, between meals, you may catch her eating any number of things that aren't on her diet. Her comment is that she'll pay for her indiscretion. Back to my theory. If you have to brush, floss and rinse, it just isn't worth it.

With my diet, there's no limitation on what can be consumed. There are no "shalt nots." The rule is plain and simple--with only one line: After eating, brush, floss and rinse.

BOX OF CHOCOLATES

It was a difficult nine days. However, I persevered, was diligent, faithful, persistent, kept my eye on the ball, my shoulder to the wheel, my nose to the grindstone--and now I am proud to tell you that I've been triumphant. The chocolates are gone! Finished, devoured, extinct, caput. They are now on my hips, tummy and thighs. The three-pound box of chocolates now weighs 23½ pounds on me--and mostly in one blob. Next time, I'm going for the gusto and eat all of them at once!

Unfortunately, there was not one unlikeable chocolate in the box. I hid the box, put it in a high place that was next to impossible to reach. I had to get the step stool each time the chocolate urge hit--which was often. Getting the step stool was a pain in the neck, so I just put the chocolates on the kitchen counter to keep them handy--after I made every possible effort to forget about them--and even went to the extreme of filling my time with meaningful activities. Still, in the end (sorry about the pun), I overcame every obstacle and persisted until every chocolate was gone.

The clothes that I already had difficulty fastening around me now chuckled out loud as soon as I touched them to consider their wear ability. The few items that did make it totally around the challenging middle looked like a tent. There's an expression that "What goes around still fits." Not much of my wardrobe fell into that category.

The three-pound box of chocolates that translated itself to 23½ pounds after entering my body had, and has, no redeeming grace. There is absolutely nothing good that can be said about chocolate. Many people are allergic to chocolate. Some cannot handle the calcium that's in the chocolate. All are transformed by the chocolate. Chocolate is a drug--different in design from cocaine and others of that ilk; nonetheless, it's a drug. It's addictive and harmful to health.

It causes muscle cramps and headaches. It's instrumental in the development of kidney stones and everyone knows it creates a high. It's just that chocolate feels so good for the moment. Actually, one good thing can be said for chocolate-- it, like nothing else, lives up to its full potential of satisfying at the moment and multiplying thereafter forever more.

When I eat chocolate, I ask myself, "What's in it for me?" Along about the fifth piece, I realize that the answer is 84 pounds. Still, there's the federal law that kicks in big time. It states something to the effect that if a box of chocolates is in a room, it's better to eat every piece in one day and see how much fat can be added to one's bulk rather than to spread them out over several days--because the same bulk, or more, will be added with the same or less pleasure--assuming you live until the next day to enjoy the pleasure.

Since there are uncertainties in life about whether or not anyone will be around tomorrow and about the lifetime effect of chocolate if spread out over several days or weeks, it's best to consume the entire box--cardboard and all--as quickly as possible and enjoy the sure thing.

CLEANING THE KITCHEN FLOOR

We cleaned our home today--well, mostly the kitchen, and primarily the kitchen floor. We slaved for hours and hours to bring it up to par. Actually, when I say "we," that isn't exactly what I mean. It may not have been hours and hours--and I didn't say we did it without taking a nap in between. Let me explain.

Hal went downstairs to put a letter into the mail slot. When he put his shoes on, I knew he planned to do more than go to the lobby to mail the letter. I knew it might be awhile before I saw him again. It was.

So, back to the beginning. I slaved for hours cleaning the kitchen, including the cabinets. Okaaay, it wasn't hours. It was only 15 minutes, but I worked so fast that I accomplished as much as some might in hours. I washed all of the cabinets. That's the kind we have--ones that can be washed. Yes, we knew about the other kind and decided they won't work for us. Been there, done that. We need washable cabinets because at least one person in our home has been known to spill or splash on them.

Anyway, I washed the doors and sides inside and out. Noooo, I didn't say shelves. We do shelves just in the even numbered years and only the bottom shelf in each cabinet then because it's the only one that really shows to the naked eye (or covered eye, either, for that matter). I cleaned the counter top, the outside of the refrigerator, the stove, and the dishwasher. I'm telling you in detail because we don't do this every week. If you do, you shouldn't be reading this; if you don't, you understand.

The answer is, "I don't know." The question is, "How do the sides of the cabinets get dirty when no one is there to dirty them?" The fact is we've been gone more than we've been here, and there's simply no excuse for dirt or spills. Anyway, they're clean now. Or, at least, they were at 9:15 this morning. And so was the sink--both bowls.

I want to suggest to you that you plan your total day--maybe the rest of your life--before you clean the kitchen sink. What good is it going to do to clean the sink if you scrub the floor next, or if you're going to eat again that day, or if you splash water on it? Well, I did it backward, but it looked great for a few minutes.

Then Hal returned. I was ready for him. I had swept the floor. It's tile.

Sixteen-inch square tile laid on the diagonal. Eighty-four miles of it. Please remember that. The tile is whitish. The grout is whitish. When the tile people suggested a darker grout, I chose the white grout.

The grout was sealed so it wouldn't discolor. Now that you know all of this, be prepared for a quiz later on--and besides, you really should focus when I'm talking because it's very rude not to. Now, back to the grout.

The scrub pail was ready for Hal. The mop was placed into his expectant hand. The cleaning product for the floor, which shall remain nameless for reasons you'll determine later, was on the counter top for him to measure. A very large measuring cup was beside it so the amount of water mixed with the cleaner could also be measured accurately.

At this point, you need to realize that I have never, not even one time in my married life, cleaned a floor with a mop. Hal, on the other hand, likes to use a string mop. What a string mop does is put a lot of water on the floor that can never, ever in this life be dried. Hal and I have had this discussion before. With a string mop, he can push the dirt onto the baseboards and into the corners, making the floor look cleaner in the middle and the baseboards dirtier.

Notwithstanding my admonitions about not buying a string mop because I don't like it, Hal began admiring them. I discouraged the purchase. He succumbed to my desires--well, mainly because I told him his life would be worthless if he were to buy it... Whew! That was close. Then, one day, he went shopping without me. Yes, he did, and he bought it.

When he brought it in the door, I told him that if he ever in this life used a string mop in our new home, I would tighten the handle that was now curved and looped around his neck.

The string mop was put into the trash chute--when Hal wasn't looking. Oh, surely I've told you about the trash chute that's the love of our life and the reason we bought the condo and over which Hal and I have a contest each day to see who can frequent it the most often with the trash bag that may not even need to be emptied because it's so nice not to have to be in the rain or the snow to take the trash out and the trash is put into bags that we get for free from the grocery store with groceries in them. And that was the end of the string mop.

But, I digress. We now have a self-squeezing sponge mop. Actually, three of them. I can't explain this. Just take my word for it that strange things happen to Hal when he's in the grocery store. Anyway, all of them are the type that can be squeezed so dry you almost don't have any water at all. Now, that's my kind of mop--if I were going to use a mop, which I'm not because that's not the way to clean a floor. And also because I now have a retired Hal who needs to feel important and who, therefore, mops the floor.

I may not have told you, but Hal has a thing about water. He thinks the more you use, the more often you use it and the more you splash it and/or leave it on flat surfaces, the better life is. I, on the other hand, cannot stand a drop of water on the counter top. Indeed, I can't stand water that stands longer that three seconds anywhere. When I mop, which I don't because I scrub on my hands and knees, but if I did, and when

21

I do scrub, there is never ever any water left on the floor because I dry it immediately with paper towels.

When Hal mops, he would let the water stand 'til the last trumpet sounds if I didn't come along and tell him it has to be dried that second. Well, he still doesn't dry it--but I continue to tell him.

He was instructed about how to scrub the kitchen floor, and he set about doing the chore in a diligent manner. Despite the wonderful quality the mop possessed of squeezing the water from the sponge, Hal still managed to leave a great deal on the floor. When he finished, he commented that the grout didn't look clean. I agreed and said there were some tiles that seemed to be a different color than I remembered them originally.

So I got on my hands and knees with my knee pads on--the ones Hal gave me for our first Christmas in our condo so I could seal the grout on my hands and knees--took some cleanser and a sponge. There was a miraculous difference in the tiles where I was working which were in the bathrooms and everywhere except the kitchen.

Hal was in the kitchen, and I still can't believe what I saw. It was a Kodak moment--one to remember and savor during the bad times. He was treading water that he left on the floor when he cleaned it with a mop, *but here he was, on his hands and knees* cleaning the tile and the grout.

When I die, I want my tombstone to read, "He did it for her."

THE GREAT RESEARCH
OR A BIRD IN THE BUSH
IS WORTHLESS

In another life, I had a license plate that read, "I Like Me." Usually, I did like me--and still do. Usually, I had some degree of organization and usually, there was some sort of accomplishment to be reviewed at the end of the day--a definite need of mine. Retirement is a new world to us, and we're not at all sure that we like the way time passes through our hands. So, to occupy my time well, I started a project--a computer research project that involved hypothetical money.

While I knew it would not be without it's own set of rules and problems, I learned how to research financial matters (the stock market) on the Internet. Having an addictive personality, I knew what could happen--that I could research the same subject for days, finding new data in new ways. I researched for days--and weeks. This particular exercise was on the subject of investments. In fact, you may want to tune out now before you learn more than you ever wanted to know on this subject. Mutual Funds that had performed the absolute best last year, year-to-date for this year, in the seventeenth century, and so on back to the creation were discovered and noted.

Well, now, don't take that information lightly. It didn't just fall down from heaven. I had to work at it, sifting through various sources, finding many, many funds and then analyzing them. There were many factors to consider before a group would be considered worthy for my collection of names.

It was from this vast array of information that the "List of Twenty-five" absolute top funds was established. I mean prime. The cream of the crop. Never mind what some of the world's best analysts recommended. They had made a few mistakes this year that I didn't plan to forgive quickly--and I

23

believed that my research was as reliable as theirs. As a matter of fact, mine was actually infallible! I'm talking about selecting funds that grew by more than 100% last year and more than 50% so far this year.

So, I, in my infinite wisdom, made a list, entering the names of the funds into a program in my computer. This program provided day-to-day change in value, as well as percent of growth/decline. Of course, there weren't any declines in funds on the "List of Twenty-five."

By this time, the research file was thick. You see, in my research, I printed data about each fund. If you think this was a ten or twenty minute project, please think another time or two. We're talking days of toil--and evaluation. This would be the list that even the most savvy of analysts and investors would envy. People would likely pay big money to have access to these names. And all it cost me was weeks of time and two ink cartridges.

You realize, of course, that the list of twenty-five funds had to be entered in my computerized program as if money was invested in each fund. I chose to invest $10,000 in each fund. Please bear in mind this was hypothetical money. After all, this portfolio represented $250,000 of new investments.

Within days, the twenty-five funds grew from $250,000.00 to $297,062.59. That was a hypothetical profit of $47,062.59 in sixteen business days. Please pause for a moment here to get the full impact of that last sentence. Are you impressed with my skill and expertise?

Because the growth was so stupendous, I realized that my genius was to be commended and congratulated. I would share my secrets with the world. For a price.

The high I experienced was higher than most of my highs. It was all I could think and obsess about. It was the last thing checked at night and the first thing in the morning. I made my lists in various formats. It was a time to remember and in which to revel--which I did.

Hal must have developed a streak of envy because he finally told me that he didn't want to hear about hypothetical money any more. Oh, well, it would just be his loss--not to share my hypothetical joy, that is.

A few weeks later, the tide turned dramatically. The "List of Twenty-five" funds was about $65,000 in the hole! It was almost the end of life as I knew it. My spirits were dampened. It was without a doubt the most devastating thing that had ever happened to me in my hypothetical life. To top off my despair, Hal chose this time to tell me that I should not have spent our hypothetical fortune. What?

I, who felt so generous during the days of our hypothetical prosperity, I who had spent the hypothetical gains, as well as anticipated future gains, now had to reevaluate life. The easily made gain of $47,062.59 in only sixteen working days was gone.

Please, I know about the addiction support groups. Surely you can understand my situation and realize there really wasn't time for me to attend one of them because I was on the Internet. Besides, how could a person of my genius attend a support group?!

AN OXFORD CLOTH SHIRT

Whenever we're going out for a casual event, Hal will almost always ask me to choose a shirt for him. Once in awhile, I'm involved in (1) dressing myself, (2) taking a shower, (3) cleaning up the kitchen, (4) writing a story or (5) researching the Internet. I know that it's hard for you to believe that I have anything to do except run when he calls, but sometimes I do. I always respond, "Wear the blue, Oxford cloth, short-sleeve dress shirt with no tie or jacket."

So, Hal will put on a shirt that isn't blue, doesn't have short sleeves, will put a tie on, have his jacket in hand and be ready to go.

Very gently, I suggest to him that he take the shirt off and wear the blue, short-sleeve shirt that I'm handing him. And he does it.

Then, he takes the one he had on for 23 seconds and puts it into the dirty clothes hamper! Yes, he does; I'm not kidding you.

It took a while for me to figure out how he could have 12 dress shirts in the wash each week. And then one day the light bulb went on, and I had a new perspective on life.

Now, I just go to the hamper, pull out the shirt, put it on a hanger, button the top button and put the shirt back into his closet. No, I don't take the ones he's actually worn and put them back on a hanger! You should be ashamed of yourselves to even think such a thing.

Granted, the washing part is nothing--and the ironing part isn't much more. I've finally found a shirt for Hal to wear that requires absolutely no ironing except to press a crease in the sleeve. Then the shirt looks as if it's been ironed when it hasn't been--except for the crease.

27

I buy shirts at K-Mart. They cost $9.95 on sale. I have to do this because Hal uses his shirts mostly to keep his chest and tummy from getting food spilled on them. You see, he sits with his chair pushed about three feet away from the table. Well, actually, I guess he has to. Otherwise, the table and his tummy might collide.

Three feet is a long way to carry spaghetti to get it into his mouth without dripping tomato sauce. While I realize Hal could lean his bod toward the table, that isn't the way he does it. It isn't the way any man does it. It's the way a woman does it.

Sometimes Hal stands at the kitchen counter and eats a tomato. When he does this, he arches his back and throws his shoulders into the shape of an "S." That makes his mouth farther from his hands than usual. As a result, the tomato is apt to hit more of his shirt than his mouth--not to mention the counter and the floor.

This is not a new phenomenon. Still, it hasn't happened all of his adult life. I believe it's been more of an occurrence in, say, the last four or five years. In fact, I believe the trend is directly proportional with a weight gain, much of which has settled directly below the chest.

The blue Oxford cloth shirt is perfect--easy to launder--and requires just a crease on the sleeve.

IN CASE OF
A HURRICANE

In the early part of June articles are published about how to prepare for a hurricane. In Florida, there's no "if" in front of the word hurricane. It isn't an "iffy situation," and food, medical, cleaning and disinfecting supplies may be needed.

It's a given that hurricanes will be all around. The people who talk about hurricanes will continue talking until they think of something to say. If an announcement is made at 4:00 p.m., that same announcement will be made for ten more hours--even when the hurricane is definitely not a threat. I realize that these people are simply doing their job. On the other hand, stand in our shoes. When do we really begin to pay attention?

Those who warn us in advance, well before the season begins, say that now is the exact moment to take action. In addition to planning for an escape route, care for animals and how to board up one's home, they talk about food and supplies we should have on hand in the event that evacuation doesn't take place but power lines are down and water is not available.

A listing of things we would need, whether staying or leaving, was printed. It was divided into categories of tools, sanitary needs, medical needs, non-prescription items, valuable papers and documents--and food.

The first thing that came to my attention was the tools. It would take a 40x40 foot storage shed to house them. If the tools are in the shed, obviously, they're not in the home. If they're in the home, there will be no room to move. Nonetheless, the list was well thought through, and we're paying attention to it.

The recommended sanitary, medical and non-prescription needs that were listed were sufficient to fill an attic--if a person had one. Hey, we live in a condo. We can't put everything on the kitchen counter!

It was the food, however, that really interested me. The writer spoke about having non-perishables such as canned tuna and other meats, peanut butter, vegetables and fruits. Hal could have created this list.

When we moved, we had enough canned items to last a family of eight, stranded on a deserted island for years. We had 57 cans of tuna, 43 cans of Vienna Sausage, 12 jars of peanut butter and six boxes of raisins that were packaged during the great depression. Oh, that isn't all. We had other things, too. You just don't want to hear about them.

At the present time, we have more canned Sprite and Mountain Dew than can be consumed before the last trumpet sounds.

The tuna that's in the back of the cabinet really doesn't get rotated properly. In other words, when Hal buys 16 more cans of tuna (which he does at least twice a week because it's on sale and he has to do it), do you think for a moment that he takes the old cans of tuna and pushes them to the front, while placing the new purchases in the rear?

The date on one can of Vienna Sausage indicates that it was prepared in the year of the battle of Bull Run during the Civil War, and the poor bird who found land and was dumb enough to go back to the ark is now packaged under the label of "Noah's Dove."

There's no point is discussing the freezer because all of that food will spoil when the electricity goes off during the hurricane. There'll be no way to cook the food because there'll be no electricity, there'll be no way to dispose of the thawed food from the freezer because the disposal won't work and it can't be flushed down the toilet because the sewage will be backed up. It's going to be a sight--or should I say scent?

Just in case of emergency, however, Hal bought some extra cleaning supplies like laundry detergent, toilet bowl cleaner, ammonia, bleach and other disinfectants. They'll likely be useful--especially since there won't be any water--except the bottled stuff that's already sprung a leak.

At least we can clean the kitchen counter with diet Sprite and bleach.

ONE COMMAND AT A TIME

Regis Philbin told an audience that the reason there are fewer women contestants than men on the program *Who Wants to Be a Millionaire* is because men have the capability of clicking faster than women. That being the case, a man wouldn't be able to get any information at all on my computer which informs me in no uncertain terms that I click too fast. Let me tell you about it.

I tell the computer to cut, paste, save and print in rapid-fire order. The computer used to obey the commands, but nowadays, it often balks. When it does balk, it says that I've performed an illegal action.

When that message flashed on the screen, I was shocked. In the first place, I consider myself to be a law-abiding citizen, except for having a heavy foot when driving the car, and I was embarrassed. What had I done? Did the neighbors know? The FBI? Would I be deported? Was the computer destroyed? Would I lose my program? Would I lose the page? If so, how could I ever reconstruct the information? What did I do wrong? I'm not a criminal!

There was no warning that I was clicking too fast. I was not told to give one command at a time. I was not told that the computer was temperamental.

Some people might say that I anticipate the next moment and have already reacted before it happens. Those people might be right. As a general rule, I've finished the day before 12:00 noon. How can I do that? Because I already have a good idea of what's coming. I lived yesterday and the day before.

When Hal begins to speak, I know what the remainder of the question or statement will be. When I'm in a meeting and a person begins to make a report, I can finish the sentence and proceed to the solution before the reporter is halfway through. You might construe those facts to mean that I have a listening problem. You might construe it to mean that I have an attention disorder. You might be wrong. It's good time management. You see, I just want to get on with it. Get to the bottom line, find a solution and go to the next issue.

So it is with the computer. If, by clicking, I tell the computer to cut, paste, print and save, just do it and quit horsing around. Then we can go on to the next exercise.

The Internet is even more temperamental. It took a while for me to feel comfortable with this complicated and intricate source of information. I was gentle and cautious. You see, I was afraid that when I clicked I would leave the area were I currently was, where I was feeling comfortable, for an unknown where I might never experience a sense of security again. Not only that, I might not find my way back to where I was and the data that was deemed to be glorious and wonderful.

What a dilemma. I was wrong if I did and wrong if I didn't. So, when in doubt, do. And I did--do. Click.

Sometimes when I clicked, I didn't like what was happening--or I changed my mind en route. However, being a faster clicker than the women in the study that Regis cited, my clicks were construed as presenting conflicting messages, and the computer said to heck with it and quit working. It sent me a message, in no uncertain terms, that I was out. Oh You Tee, OUT! Finished. Caput. No more. So long, good to know you. Sayonara. Don't come back.

The more I clicked, the more I cajoled, the more I repented, the more stubborn and obstreperous the computer became. The computer is a male!!! It must be because it always has to be right. I lost. Every time. It said the server couldn't be found and if it could, it wouldn't serve me because I clicked too much, too fast and too often.

Listen, I'm not young. I've got to live fast because I don't know how many more good clicking years I've got. But aside from that thought, how does the computer react to a male who can click faster than I can?

In case you think I need a new computer with a faster speed, just let me remind you that our computer is only three months old and was state-of-the-art at the time it was purchased--which in layman's terms means that it was a dinosaur by the time it hit the market.

There's more to this story. The computer punishes me. After telling me that I'm no longer welcome to use it and after kicking me off, it won't let me back on. Sometimes it teases me and let's me get part way and then kicks me off again. It's a masochist. It likes to see me suffer.

I'm beginning to think my first grade teacher had a conversation with my computer, and is trying to get even with me. That's vindictive, you know and is an attitude that's unbecoming and is probably in violation of one of the commandants.

The other reason that I think the computer is male is because a male can often take only one command at a time. For example, if I say to Hal, "Please take out the trash, close the window, turn off the light and then I'll be ready to go," nothing gets done. He can't even remember the part about "take out the trash." He jumped the track long before I said, "close the window." And don't even hope that he ever heard the part about "turn out the light."

It has taken many years of marriage for me to learn to give only one command at a time. The only trouble with this is that I'll forget the other two things I want him to do while waiting for him to do the first command.

However, if I give one command, such as, "Hal, I need your attention for one minute. Look at me and listen to me, please. Take out the trash," he probably will be able to handle it.

One of the disadvantages of that particular command is that, after taking the trash to the chute, he then goes to the landing rail and looks at the ponds for 20 minutes. By the time he comes back in, I've already closed the window, turned off the light, finished my hair, put on my face on, brushed my teeth, scrubbed the kitchen, washed a load of clothes, phoned a friend and gotten kicked off the computer. Twice.

THE JOY OF WRITING

At one time, I was employed. I liked my work so much that I could hardly wait to get up and get going. There was a wonderful office in my home. It was one where I hardly ever had to get out of my chair, regardless of what I wanted. For example, the computer with printer surrounded me--almost literally. The Fax machine was an arm's length to the left with pre-programmed numbers--for the whole world, of course. The file cabinets required that I stand only if I wanted something that was in the top two drawers. My present office is even better and I'm more addicted to my writing that I was addicted to my work in my previous life. Hal enjoys the office as much as I do, not necessarily because he shares it or because it's functional, but because it gives him a respite.

In my former life, I was in my office before breakfast. The computer was on, the fax was on, and the photocopier was warming--as I jumped in the shower.

I hurried back to the office to check for E-mail, printed it while bolting down breakfast. Back to the office to start the copying of papers that were too important not to have multiple copies of them. Then, I paused to brush my teeth. Back to the office. I simply couldn't get there fast enough, work hard enough and stay long enough. I loved it.

Now, I'm finding that I just can't wait to get to the computer and begin typing to tell you about one of my significant encounters, without the knowledge of which, your day would be incomplete. The routine is similar to the days when I worked. Or, was it work? Was it so much fun, so exhilarating, such joy that no one would dare put the label of "work" on any of my actions?

Regardless of the genuine excitement that I feel when letting words flow rapidly, I'm concerned that some of my enthusiasm may be driven by an "avoidance" motivation. You see, if a person has some degree of energy and isn't otherwise occupied, her eye may wander to the imperfections in others-- or things. That eye may see spills on the kitchen floor that would otherwise have been overlooked if the mind and hands were occupied with other thoughts.

This revelation came to me one day when Hal was urging me to get to the keyboard and begin writing. As I recall, he was trying to do some paper work. It's possible that I had asked him the same questions that I asked him every day, which are something like this.

"Did you clean up the splashed water that's on the floor?"

"Did you brush, floss and rinse?"

"Did you call Denton about fishing?"

Did you, did you, did you? Hal says about eight sentences come out in one breath. He says that's why he doesn't respond. By the time I've paused for breath to ask six more questions, he's forgotten what the first one was. At least, that's his story.

He thinks it's a good idea for me to sit at the computer and write stories all day long--from before sun up to well after sun down.

MOVE IT AGAIN' SAM

It doesn't matter where it's put today; tomorrow it will be in a different place--and after four moves, it may end up where it was to begin with. Do I really think that it's progress to move things around? Do I equate motion with positive action? Probably.

All of the screwdrivers are in one place. All 38 of them. In one drawer. In the laundry room. Except for the ones that are in my pencil-holder cup that have our company name on them. Four of them. Not four cups, four screwdrivers. It's the screwdrivers that have our company name on them. Don't even go there. I don't know why there are four of them.

I don't know why there are 38 screwdrivers in the drawer in the laundry room either. Or three hammers (or for that matter, four pressure cookers, four vacuum cleaners, two juice extractors, two hair dryers . . .).

We live in a condo where there'll be little use for any of the mentioned items. I mean, it's unlikely there'll be major construction changes taking place in this condo or that we'll need four pressure cookers at one time. I will admit that the screwdrivers have been used quite a bit since we moved--and the hammers too.There's the smallest possibility that not every screw or nail was put in the right place on the first round--but I will say that several screws and nails have been placed somewhere. Sometimes more than once in the same hole, even after it was patched because it was decided that the first decision wasn't the right decision--and then redecided that it was. By this time, we're likely on the seventh round.

Hal gave our children most of his tools. Evidently he didn't give away any of his screwdrivers. Do you know how much space is required to store 38 screwdrivers? Ok, not that much.

Still, the point is, who needs 38 screwdrivers-- Or four pressure cookers or three irons?

The screwdrivers are just one example. I could tell you about sticky tabs, hanging file tabs, binder clips or staplers and the time spent organizing, containerizing, reorganizing and recontainerizing these items. How did this happen?

They kept surfacing. Everywhere. They multiplied like hangars! How could they be packed in seven different moving boxes? Because some were on Hal's desk, some on mine, some in the kitchen drawer, some on my dresser so they'd be handy. Not the boxes, the office supplies.

Don't even mention the pads of papers. Some pads have several pages of notes like a phone number without a name, some calculations that have no meaning, a note about an appointment with an unknown person, comments from a conversation with a nameless friend and other valuable information. Those notes may be valuable some day.

You just don't understand our lifestyle if you can't comprehend the dilemma that's presented from all of the over stocking of supplies. Do you realize that enough to support a child in a developing country for the rest of time has been spent on containers to hold things like paper clips?

Regardless of all of the above, we ran out of hanging file folders. It isn't that we didn't bring enough with us on the move. Rather, it's just that we have a gift for filling files. Well, maybe the gift is really the ability to keep that which no other sane person would have in the home to begin with.

I'm pleased to inform you, however, that we believe in the sanctity of the written word. If Hal or I think a subject is sufficiently important to request a brochure, pick up a pamphlet at the stand in the hotel lobby or write a note during a conversation, we will keep the brochures and notes forever. If our children, later on, feel that the information is not worthy of their keeping it for posterity and future generations, that's their problem. They'll be the ones filling the trashcans and overfilling the refuse dumps. In the meantime, it's our obligation to move things--week after week.

I finally put the paperback books in a place that I felt was quite suitable. Later, I noticed that the books were "cluttering" another space. Since I hadn't moved the books, there could be only one other person who had done so. His explanation was that he felt he found a better location.

I, on the other hand, in my infinite wisdom, decided that it would be far superior to house three boxes of old pictures and letters in the first guest room rather than in the guest room/office.

So, I moved 28 containers to get the three boxes out of the office closet and into the guest room closet. When the job was finished and I was sweating bullets, it didn't seem like such a good idea after all. In the first place, the boxes didn't fit their new home.

Fortunately, I hadn't requested assistance in this endeavor, and I moved it all back before my roommate knew that they had been moved in the first place.

The hammer was in the fourth drawer of the laundry room last week. Two days ago it was put in the "junk drawer" in the kitchen so it would be handy in case it was needed in the kitchen. Yesterday, it was placed under the sink in the bathroom because some pictures might be hung there. Not hung under the sink--on the wall!

Today, it's considered a "tool," and it's now in the third drawer of the laundry room where tools are kept, including the 3" pencil and the scissors.

It's reached the point that when we want something, we have to turn on our personal computers that sit on our shoulders and run through the entire menu before we can even hope to remember where we last put the items for which we're searching. I didn't say that the computer functions quickly--or accurately. If we didn't move things around, however, when would the computer be stimulated?

THE OTHER CHILD

Hal's job was to paint the quarter round. He painted a few (do two qualify as a few?) 8' pieces and took a break. While on his break, he asked me to stop what I was doing to find something for him. I took off my rubber gloves (I was cleaning), changing my focus from the very important job at hand to assist him in his monumental mission which was finding something he had misplaced--though the distinct implication (accusation) was that I had touched it and made it disappear.

Hal finished his break and started painting again. There were 26 pieces of 8' quarter round. He painted a few more (again, I believe it was two) and took another break--and asked me the location of something else. This time I was in the bathroom. Whatever he needed, it was urgent, and he wasn't too keen on waiting until my bathroom duty was complete.

This was repeated two or three more times when he broke for lunch. By that time I couldn't remember where I put the scrubbing equipment or why I went to the bathroom. In fact, I didn't remember that I had even been doing either--and I couldn't find the rubber gloves to resume the job, assuming that I remembered what I was doing and wanted to resume the job. I did still know where the bathroom was located, although I couldn't remember at what stage the interruption had occurred.

I decided that we should reverse roles; I would paint and interrupt Hal--and let him try to refocus on whatever he was doing (I believe he was looking at the bay).

When the children were young, it didn't matter what I was doing and in what stage I was in doing it, they always needed something, and I interrupted my focus to take care of "the

43

something." Nothing has changed except that three of the children grew up and moved to their own homes. The child to whom I'm married didn't grow up and didn't move.

If this child wants me to eat with him, he wants me to stop whatever--even though it may take only 30 seconds to finish my task--ok, sometimes it's ten minutes. Still, I'm to quit that instant. Now, on the other hand, when I want this child to interrupt his thought process and pay attention to what I need-- like finding my glasses--that's another matter.

When I misplace my keys, it's because I'm careless and would lose my body parts if they weren't attached. When Hal misplaces his keys, it's because I'm careless and would lose my body parts if they weren't attached.

LAUNDERING MONEY

The first time I heard about laundering money, I thought it was a good idea.   Money is dirty, there's no question about that. Have you ever seen a person in a restaurant ring the cash register, thereby handling money, and then put a roll on your plate with her hands and then serve your other food?   In a department store, the sales clerk counts out your money; the bills stick together, so she wets the tip of her finger (in her mouth) to continue making change.   She's sniffling, and sneezes before being able to cover her face. Then, you touch the money--and guess what. Within a few days, you have a cold.   Hal said I was totally off track in all of this rationale because laundering money had nothing to do with cleanliness and hygiene. Still, he isn't always right.

When I originally heard about the concept, I couldn't quite imagine how the laundering process would be done. Would the money be put into the dishwasher or the washing machine? Or would it be washed by hand? Would the coins be placed in, say, a mesh bag and the bills be placed in still another mesh bag?   Would the printing on the paper fade while it washed? I guess a person wouldn't want to use bleach in the load where the paper money was being washed.

How often would the money be washed? Every day? If the paper money made it through the first wash, how many more washes would it sustain? And--even though you chose to keep your money clean, how about the next person who might not be such a clean freak as you. Would you mix that money with your clean money? It would be like putting a dirty towel back on the shelf with the clean towels.

You know how you put a shirt or blouse in the hamper to be washed every day. Would you just keep a separate wallet to carry the unwashed paper money and put the dirty money in its mesh bag to be washed when the next load was done? Of course, all of this assumes that you would have more money on hand than you needed for any given day and could afford to have some of it in the laundry basket.

If you were diligent in always putting the clothes away the minute they were washed and dried, the money, likewise, could be ironed (it might be stiff--wouldn't it--and ironing would soften it) and put in your clean, sterile wallet. If you didn't touch the clean money for any reason, it would stay clean. But, if you had a cold, had germs on your hands and then touched the money, all of your laundering would be for naught.

Well, about the time I felt that the laundering procedure was worked out in my mind for what would be best for the Ward household, I learned that "laundering" had a different meaning than the one I was applying to it.

It's interesting to me to realize that words can be used to mean so many different things. In an ordinary conversation, one can totally misunderstand every sentence because of multiple definitions. For example, take the term of "rabbit ears," which, besides meaning ears on a rabbit, also means an antenna that's attached to a television.

Well, I made a conscientious effort to learn how large amounts of money that someone wishes to hide, can be "laundered." I must say that my understanding of the procedure is minuscule to nil--or less. This may be due, in part, to the fact that I've never had enough of it to feel it needed to be hidden from the view of the federal government-- or anyone else for that matter. As a matter of fact, I thought most people liked to flaunt it if they actually had a surplus.

Still, if one is going to live in this world, she needs a little bit of general knowledge to carry on a conversation at public gatherings.

My newfound learnings were a source of inspiration and I found myself integrating terms and phrases here and there into

46

my everyday conversations--whether or not the data was germane to the discussion.

Armed with all of this knowledge about the real definition for laundered money, I reached into the dryer to remove the newly washed and dried laundry, removed three crisp one dollar bills, folded them and put them in my wallet with the "clean" money.

The lettering didn't fade and, no, I'm not going to iron the bills.

Maybe if it's ok to launder money, it's also all right to wash the ironing board cover.

DUELING VIOLETS

They were more glorious than anyone could imagine possible.   There were four of them together, each one enhancing the other and each one loaded.   Loaded with blooms, that is--and they were definitely competing with each other except for the laggards that were in still other pots. I'm talking about African Violets.

The pot in which they were so adequately accommodated is quite large and the four plants have grown to unbelievable size. The diameter of the four plants is 22 inches. Including the pot, the plants stand 16 inches tall. I believe the plants are just a common variety. These four plants have a double bloom that's purple in color, with a narrow border on the edges of white.

You see, I'm not a connoisseur of African Violets (or of anything else, for that matter), so the variety, nomenclature and identifying characteristics are totally lost on me.   I can only tell you what has happened at our home with the African Violets.

The one violet under discussion, plant one in pot one, had 76 buds on it. On just one plant! Remember, there were four African Violets in the pot, and the other three had not begun to bud. But they did, begin, that is, to bud. They'll be discussed later.

Back to the plant one in pot one with 76 buds. There was simply no question that this plant would take the prize for all time. There was no way it could be surpassed. I intended to savor every minute of the opening of the buds.

On still another occasion, there were 45 buds on one plant. That had seemed too much to be true. I feared that the weight of the 45 would be too great for the stems that were already hanging low from the weight. But this African Violet had 76 blooms! The blooms were compact, the stems stayed together, and the vision was awesome.

There was no question, pot one was now getting preferential treatment in its placement relative to the light and its visibility--and plant one was likewise being favored over plants two, three and four--although the importance of the other three plants was definitely realized because they actually heightened the beauty of plant one by filling the pot and providing support for the leaves of plant one. The leaves, you see, measured up to 10" above the soil line!

Clearly, this was the pot and the plant to enter in competition, if there was any competition and if I knew about the competition so the plant could be entered--which there wasn't and I didn't. Still, it's the thought that counts.

Remember, there were four plants in pot one. As the buds began to open on plant one in pot one, plants two, three and four began to bud.

And then, as if on a cue, plants one and two in pot two began to bud. Plant one in pot two had a multitude of buds, but I knew it would never be as spectacular as plant one in pot one with 76 buds. Even so, it was beginning to look very good.

It continued to grow larger and appeared to be in a contest with plant one in pot one. I finally feared for the health of the competitors and decided to put an end to the competition, lest the pots be destroyed along with the plants. What were they on? Steroids?

I will say at this point that pot two was showing promise, was beginning to earn more respect and it had been shifted to benefit as much as possible from the light source (which is a window--or did you already know that?), and I'll have to admit that plant one in pot two was getting preferential treatment to the other plants in pot two. Or any other pot--except pot one.

But back to the competition that I wanted to end before the health of the plants was affected. I counted the buds on plant

one in pot two. Ohmigosh. It had 103 buds! I couldn't believe it. I recounted. Why not? I'm retired now.

However, the counting was easier said than done. It's actually very hard to count that many buds without breaking a stem that's loaded with them. The stems are quite thin, brittle and fragile. I had already broken two stems on plant two in pot one (ok, so it was four stems and accounted for 53 buds).

I know you're confused at this point. Just think about how I feel! There are many pots and even more plants. Some pots are large and have four plants each. Some pots are smaller and have fewer plants. Most of the pots have plants that are doing their best. But, as you might assume, there are a few that aren't putting forth as much effort as I believe they could.

It was time for an attitude adjustment session for them. I mentioned the potential that each plant had and stressed the fact that there was the smallest possibility that each one might not have been treated equally. Still, they didn't have to get in a big huff and not even make attractive leaves.

Pure and simply, the leaves of the plants in one of the pots were not of show quality, and their lackadaisical attitude about blooming was not acceptable. I told them I knew they could do better and they had three weeks to perform a total turn around or they would be history. While you may think that I was too stern, I made a big deal out of telling them they could be anything they chose to be.

They could choose to be number one or they could choose to goof off. The way in which they took care of their foliage and absorbed the valuable nutrients that were provided for them was an individual decision. I told them that what they did at this point in their lives would affect them as they aged and might make the difference in a pleasant retirement versus a shortened life or a lack luster existence now as well as in their later years.

My final statement was that I could guarantee a shortened life if they didn't begin to show a distinct improvement-- because there were other rooted leaves just waiting for their chance to be planted in a pot.

The four plants in pot three took the motivational speech seriously. There was a remarkable change. The color of the leaves improved and they began to bud, not only acceptably, but also prolifically. Needless to say, they still didn't appear to have the zest that plants one in pots one and two had exhibited--nor did they seem to possess the same competitive attitude as the plants in pots one and two.

Still, it appeared as if all four plants in pot three were making an effort and might be experiencing handicapping conditions of some sort that would make me appear intolerant if I were to be too judgmental with them. In fact, all four of the plants were actually doing a remarkable turn around, whereas plants three and four in pots one and two were showing no great budding ability--until the plants in pot three began to show their colors.

My fear, before the last burst of energy, was that they were feeling depressed and needed more medical attention that I am qualified, or willing, to provide. Now that there has been a distinct improvement in the apparent effort that is being exerted, I may be more inclined to extend additional care and expertise to nurse them to the position of being a bronze medallist.

The expended effort has been not only commendable, but also exemplary and the plants are now filled with almost as many buds as their momma. In addition, they have adapted well to the community, treat others with dignity, provide for their young and pay their bills.

Not every plant can be a star--fortunately because otherwise the space allocated for the many pots of African Violets would simply be insufficient and the only other space

that they might occupy is where Hal presently does his paper work.

If a choice had to be made between African Violets and Hal, well....

KERNELS THAT DIDN'T

Have you ever watched through the window of the microwave and marveled at the way the bag of popcorn swells as the kernels start popping? The bag gets larger and larger-- and the kernels pop and pop. Then the time is up. The game is over. Either the kernels performed or they didn't. You know how some of those kernels never quite made it through the popping process? That's always bothered me, so I decided to do something about it.

Maybe their lack of success was because they got nervous and couldn't work well under the pressure of a time limitation. Or, maybe the kernels just didn't have the same capability to function as some of the ones that did. You know deep down in your heart that not everything is truly created equally.

Or, just suppose the kernels were in the wrong place at the wrong time--like in the center of the bag and, therefore, didn't get as much heat as the kernels on the perimeter of the heap. The kernels in the center wouldn't have had a chance to fulfill their potential. They might have been just as capable and just as talented--maybe even gifted--and yet didn't have the same set of environmental circumstances as the other kernels.

They might have had parents who never encouraged them to push their way to the top.

In every bag of popcorn, there are perhaps a dozen or maybe two dozen kernels that never have the pleasure of total fulfillment in life. Can you put yourself in that bag and realize how devastating it must be to be one of the kernels that was too pooped to pop when the microwave stopped? Can you really feel the pain those kernels felt? Have you done anything to ease that pain?

Well, I did. I turned the microwave back on for a few more seconds. It's true there was a small chance that one of the first kernels to pop might burn. I felt that was a risk I would have to take for the greater good of the two dozen or so kernels that had never had a break in life. The few kernels that popped first were likely the cheerleaders and the football stars who had already had their day in the sun--bag, excuse me.

Now, you might be thinking that it didn't make any difference one way or the other because the kernels were a dead duck anyway. If they popped, they were doomed; if they didn't, they were doomed. So what difference did it make?

Well, to me, it makes a difference. Just think about it. If you never even had the chance to pop, would it make a difference to you if you were given that special chance and then if the person consuming the popcorn enjoyed eating you more than any of the other popped kernels? I mean, it's a matter of opportunity, of stature, of position.

You know, you wouldn't be worth squat as a human resources manager if you can't even put yourself in the bag of a popcorn kernel.

BRIDGES

As long as I can remember I've disliked bridges. Especially if the bridge is longer than a car length. Or shorter than a car length. Certainly, I dislike it if it's high. Or if it's flat and low. I dislike on and off ramps for the same reasons. The advantage of the ramp over that of a bridge is it may be shorter than a major bridge. A bridge that's half the length of a car, completely flat and only three feet above whatever it spans is enough to cause me great anxiety and nightmares.

So, here we are, in Florida where bridges cover more space than the dry land. There are bridges (ramps) on and off the highways; there are bridges over drainage ditches, bridges over canals, bridges over lakes, bridges over inlets and bridges over bays. There are bridges that are very short and bridges that are more than six miles in length. There are bridges that are low and bridges that are as high as a seventeen-story building. I, who can't deal with bridges, have to be on at least three to go across the street.

The west coast of Florida doesn't have much besides bridges. The east coast too. And there are plenty of bridges in between the two coasts. In short, there is water everywhere in Florida, but not a drop to drink or water the grass-- during times of drought.

Walt Disney looked at Central Florida, decided that he could take swamp land and make something beautiful. And he did. I, on the other hand, would have envisioned the need for a bridge and left the state forever. Mr. Disney probably wasn't afraid of bridges because he built plenty of them where he built Disney World, Epcot Center and all of the rest of his creation.

Believe me when I say you can't go across the street without using a bridge that's been built over something. Now, concentrate with me. Can you imagine a person who dislikes bridges so intensely that the nervous tension almost strangles her, moving to Florida, which is 90% bridges? I never said I was smart.

One of the most memorable experiences of my life involved a bridge. This is the way I remember that day of almost 20 years ago.

I was driving east from Washington, D.C., headed for Salisbury, Maryland. To get there, I had to cross the Chesapeake Bay Bridge. I was at the bridge before I realized I was there. I was on the bridge. There was no hesitating. There was no turning around. I was on the bridge. The bridge was higher than it used to be. It was also longer. And I was on it headed east. It was a two-lane bridge that had a side rail three inches high on the right side--and the left side. It was a two-lane bridge that I could see through and view the water below.

There was a magnet of enormous strength all along the side rails on the right, pulling my car over the rail. There was also a magnet of equal strength on the left rail just in case I decided to change from the right to the left lane. I felt myself hurtling into space. I was not going to make it across!

I can't swim. I was going to drown right smack in the middle of this high bridge with two-inch guard rails that were magnetized and pulling me over--hurtling me into space where I would have a heart attack before I drowned. There were no other cars on the bridge to help me when I had the heart attack and drowned on the bridge that was seven million miles high.

I began reciting the Twenty-third Psalm. Granted, I was using my paraphrased version. What I said was something like this. The Lord is my shepherd. I have everything I need-- EXCEPT my car is on a bridge that is seven million miles high and twice that long. He leads me beside the still waters and also on top of them--in the middle of the two lanes, far away from the water in which I'm going to drown if I don't die first from a heart attack or from hurtling through space. The Lord puts confidence into my mind that the magnetic rail will not pull me over but, if it does, he will save me and put me back on the bridge again. God's goodness and mercy are with me right now and he needs to calm my soul and restore my peace of mind--right this minute, please.

This was a prayer, not just a recitation. I prayed it once, twice, three times, four times. On the ninety-third time, I reached the end of the bridge. I made it.

The man at the toll booth of the Florida Sunshine Skyway Bridge near St. Petersburg brought me back to the moment at hand by yelling at me that I was in the wrong lane. I asked him if he wanted me to back up with three blocks of traffic behind me and go through the correct one.

He didn't know where I'd been visiting as I drove into the wrong toll booth.

crossed, not knowing if I could reach the bathroom soon enough, but the laughter wouldn't stop. The more I laughed--silently--the more Hal uttered expletives. Sprinkled amongst his choice words, he kept repeating, "I'll get you for this."

You may think at this point that it was my fault that the tomato was on the back seat. Rest assured it was not. Hal is the one who buys pounds and pounds of tomatoes at a time. We can only assume that a tomato fell out of the bag and reposed itself on the seat, waiting to be rescued and later sliced for dinner. This tomato, however, was to die a different type of death. Almost a more lethal one, if you will, than by being sliced and served.

After cleaning Hal and the back seat of the car, I remembered a rhyme from childhood and began to chant it.

A peanut sat on the railroad track.

Its heart was all a flutter.

When down the track came a choo choo train--

Toot, toot, peanut butter.

It seemed to me that there were similarities in the peanut on the railroad tract and a tomato under Hal's ampleness.

SCUFFED SHOES

You've seen children with scuffed shoes--and thought it was no wonder because of their level of activity. After all, even a prissy little girl with a cute dress and her white Mary Jane shoes is apt to take a few minutes to climb a tree. When she does, that's just about the end of those shoes. Of course, children these days more likely wear sneakers instead of a dress shoe. Have you seen the little boy who's dressed in a suit with a tie and has on a pair of clunker sneakers? The shoes may be new when you look at him on Sunday morning. By dinner time, they'll likely be shredded. How does this happen? Well, again, with a child, it's understandable. But what about men--especially my man--and scuffed shoes, and what about my need for perfectly polished and shined shoes?

My Hal has always had a way of scuffing the toes of his shoes. This seemed impossible unless he was spending a considerable amount of time on his hands and knees doing something. I know that he doesn't spend any time in this position when he's at home. I thought that on occasion he might be as he worked in the warehouse of our business. Our son, Richard, said it wasn't apt to happen.

Richard said men scuff their shoes while sitting at their desk. He says that women sit very prim and proper with their feet flat on the floor, near the front of their chair, whereas men stretch their feet out the distance of the desk and rub the shoes against parts of it. The fact that men and women are different has been documented. Still, I don't remember hearing this difference.

I believe that men do strange things with their feet when driving a car. I believe that the size of the shoe for many men is such that it stretches too far forward and too far behind the gas pedal. I believe that my man drives with the right side of his right shoe on the floorboard carpet--instead of the sole of the shoe--thus scuffing or making a light colored shoe look black. This action includes the toe of the shoe as well as the heel.

Women, on the other hand, either change into driving shoes or pad the area where the heel of the shoe will go when driving so the shoe won't be scuffed. Actually, just a few women do that. The others have shoes with scuff marks on the back of them.

Still, how can one account for a man's left shoe being scuffed? Well, I don't have a reason for that. The only thing I know is that I can't stand scuffed shoes and I can't stand to see light colored shoes that are dirty. I'm so affected by this that I don't even want to *see* a pair of shoes that has scuff marks or black marks. I certainly don't want Hal or me to wear shoes in that condition.

Before a pair of shoes can be worn in our family, the shoes must first be polished three times with a "neutral" polish to protect against water marks, spills and dirty marks--or they must be treated with Jubilee Kitchen Wax and Cleaner--a process that does the same thing. At the first sign of a scuff or dirty mark, the shoes must be retreated.

This need for perfect shoes comes from my early childhood. My parents thought it was one of the ways a man or woman looked like a gentleman or lady.

Because of the way Hal holds his foot when he drives, we came up with the idea of his wearing a surgical type of bootie over his shoes (ok, I came up with the idea). Oh my goodness, it was wonderful. The first day. He wore the bootie and didn't mess up his shoes. The second day, he remembered part of the time. By the third day, he couldn't find the bootie. It was still a good idea.

With women, one of the greatest problem is that heels sometimes get caught in the sidewalk, the curb or in cracks.

And chairs that are on rollers, such as those used in an office, take a bite out of the shoe that can never be totally repaired. Office chairs really should be ashamed.

When I polish shoes, I line them up--like soldiers--and begin to apply the polish. By the time polish is applied to the last shoe, the first one is almost dry. Not quite dry enough, though, to shine. I have to wait. The shoes strut a bit, and each one vies to be first in line for the buffing process. And then I shine with a nylon hose over the bristles of the brush. "Here I come, babies. Now sparkle for me," I tell them.

Ohmigosh they do! Hal comes looking for me to determine what the noise is about. The shoes are singing, "I'm just so happy that I can't sit down." Hal really doesn't understand the concept of shiny shoes. Well, he will when he realizes that he isn't allowed to wear them because they look too good to be messed up. My own personal shoes are a sight to behold. If the chair attacks them this week, it will certainly be in trouble.

It takes so little to light up my life.

LEARNING TO PLAY THE GUITAR

Some people have a unique way of filling two-thirds of the vacant space--all at once, regardless of where their beings actually are. Hal is one of these people, when he makes every sound imaginable--and especially when he was learning to pay the guitar.

While I admit that I can use two computers at once and can flit from chair to chair to handle the interests that are being addressed on the computers, I do so without making a sound--except for the pressing of keys--which do make some noise.

I don't talk when I'm writing, I don't talk when I'm on the Internet, I only talk--a lot--when I'm telling Hal what to do or when I'm in a social setting--or when I'm waxing eloquently on a subject for which my opinion will undoubtedly be needed.

Hal, on the other hand, talks to the computer and to printed instructions. His conversations go something like this:

"Let's see, now, this says that I should attach "C" to "A" and then wrap "D" around my ankle while I stand on my head tightening the "G" string. If I speak into the microphone, the guitar can be tuned by adjusting in accordance with negative or positive. That doesn't make any sense. These instructions are wrong. How can you wrap "G" around "Z" and not end up with "B"? Ok, now, this has been turned up, this is adjusted and this is on the left, but there's no sound. So, I'll just get under the desk and see if something is loose and adjust it...."

There's no end to it. Actually, while I put in punctuation, Hal doesn't speak with punctuation--except when he interrupts his mutters to ask if I know where it was put when it was removed.

Before I even answer the question, I should point out that for Hal to get under the desk to fight with all the cords that repose there takes a bit of doing. Getting out is even more interesting. That's just about the grand total of his exercise for any given week--under the desk one time.

Now, to answer the question--no, I don't know where it was put because I don't yet know what it is, and I don't know what it was removed from--or when.

Then Hal begins to whistle--not softly. He's exuberant. He whistles well, and I'm pleased that he's happy. I'm not pleased that he's whistling in my ear while I'm concentrating. I insert my earplugs.

The talking and whistling continue. Hal is in his chair, then under the desk, he pulls out the computer tower (please note that he does not push the tower back--ever), he's back in his chair, he hums, then whistles. I can still hear him through my ear plugs.

He goes to the closet, rummages, removes things and puts them on the bed, the couch, the table, the floor. He does *not* put them back. Next, he's in the laundry room, looking in the storage drawers there. He doesn't close the drawers. I don't need to look; I know that he doesn't close the drawers.

He connects the microphone finally (after running to Staples to get another one because he thinks the first one is defective) and begins to strum the guitar to tune it. He strums the same string a few times. Actually, 83 times. Then he strums another string, talking all the while to the computer and the guitar.

There's much to be said about talking to a computer or the guitar. Neither one talks back.

If Hal should ever get the guitar tuned, he's going to use a CD in his computer to learn to play it. I can hear it now--Jesu, Joy of Man's Desiring. Je, Je, Je, Je, Je....

I can hardly wait until the lessons begin!

WATER SAVING THEORIES

You've heard and read about the devices to make a shower a water saver, how to make a toilet a water saver, how to save water with the dishwasher, the washing machine and even the hose that's used to water the plants. In our condo, every appliance possible is a water saver and/or an electricity saver. Not that it was our choice, but the condo is new and that's the way things are built now. On the surface, that's very pleasing because it's more economical to live that way and, hopefully, the environment will benefit from all of this saving. But a water saving toilet?

Recently, when we were in a hotel, where there was not a water saving device in the shower, the water flowed graciously, gloriously, generously. It was delightful.

As wonderful as it was, however, it did not equal the toilet. When it flushed, it flushed! There was a mighty whoosh. It was the most wonderful sound we'd heard for a long time.

As indelicate as this subject is, I simply must tell you that our water saving toilets are a thorn in our side, a pain in the kididlehopper, an irritation that's present with us always, every day, several times a day. There is only one way around it--and that's to go to McDonald's when we have the urge. No, no, I'm only kidding. There really is an alternative.

You see, our toilets are constantly stopping up--unless we flush four times during every visit. Either way, if we do or don't, the end result is the same--I mean as far as water is concerned. At least four flushes. Of course, the experts on this water saving subject, might argue that any toilet that holds only a tablespoon of water to begin with is still less of a water guzzler with four flushes than a nonwater saver with one flush.

It had to be a male who thought up the wing-ding water saving toilet in the first place. A woman could never possibly be that stupid! Puhleeze, this isn't the place to save water or money.

Almost all women know how to save water. Women don't let the water run while brushing their teeth; men do. Women don't leave gallons of water on the floor when cleaning it; men do. Women don't run water needlessly when rinsing dishes; men do.

While we're waiting for women to correct such ridiculous things as a water saving toilet, we'll end up with a water shortage more severe than we've ever known before. I suspect that we use three times as much water as we would if the toilet were not a water saver.

There was an ad in today's newspaper that read, "You can get a new toilet for only $50.00 fully installed . . .." I guess so. There's probably a big market out there in old, non-water saving toilets. Our plumber told us he waited a long time to replace a water saving toilet in his home with one that was not a water saver--and quickly put it in his home. I bet those old toilets will sell on the secondary market for at least $1,000.00. I'm calling our plumber later today to put our name in for three of them.

Our plumber said prior to the time when he rescued a toilet from the demolition hammer, it was embarrassing for him to have to admit that he didn't have an acceptable pot to bleep in.

ADDICTIONS

I've spoken before about addictions. We have many of them. Some people want to hide theirs, sweep them under the rug, put on a brave exterior and pretend they don't exist. Not us. We're open about ours. We describe them, discuss the ramifications, evaluate the cause of them and determine the need for healing--especially if the addiction isn't mine.

The discussion today will deal with only one addiction. It will belong to Hal. Did you think we'd be discussing someone else?

Hal's addiction is shopping--for groceries--not just food, but also anything that can be bought at the grocery store--that can't outrun him.

He has shopped for our groceries for the last 15 or 20 years. He doesn't take a list. He doesn't need one. He's too good at it to use a list. Hal walks up and down the aisles and rakes everything he can reach on the shelves into his cart. He may need more than one. He doesn't do this on a quarterly or monthly basis; he doesn't do this on a weekly basis; he does it daily. *Daily.* Sometimes *two* or *three times* in one day!

At one time, we had two upright freezers. All were full. When they had to be defrosted, Hal threw away most of the food. Some of it was beyond recognition. It didn't matter what items were placed back into the freezer, they would soon be hidden by the latest purchases.

He doesn't buy one, feeling that if one will be good, some will be better, many will be best and big will be the frosting on the cake. It doesn't matter whether or not he likes the food, although he is partial to some things. It does matter whether or not it's on sale. There's a little known federal law that says if an item is on sale, you must buy it if you're in the store and if you can possibly get the item to fit into the shopping cart. If you don't do it, it's a federal offense. If you don't know about the law, it isn't.

We used to have storage everywhere. If Hal bought 10 cans of Cream of Mushroom Soup, it wasn't the end of the world. The time he bought 25, however, it almost was--for him.

Hal doesn't just buy food. For example, he buys cleaning supplies.

Whether or not they're the brand I like, he buys--a lot. At one time, we had 15 very large size containers of laundry detergent. He didn't buy all of them at once. Rather, he bought one or two every time he went to the store and saw what he presumed was a sale. It was the federal law, you know. The laundry shelf was full to the point there wasn't any room for bleach or other products. It took three years to use all of them.

One day Hal took a package from the freezer. Other packages shifted. He couldn't get the door closed. By taking everything out of the freezer, I was able to rearrange and get it all back in--after throwing away seven packages of unrecognizable food.

There were eight bags and five boxes of frozen cauliflower with or without broccoli, 12 packages of frozen chicken breasts, nine of pork chops and six of ground meat.

The standard lecture was administered. Hal was told that he wasn't allowed to go to the store for at least a week. And then, he had to go with a list of things that were needed. The very next day he went out the door with the excuse that he needed to go to the Post Office. Do you have any idea where else he went? You're right--and he bought a 15-pound package of ground meat. It was on sale.

He's partial to certain stores. He goes first to the one farthest away and works his way back. On a good day, he'll hit five grocery stores, three fresh produce markets, two drug stores and the 7-11.

Hal says I'm too bossy. When I, in a very calm voice, advised him that he had spent $650 for groceries last month, he said, "Ok, I'll be more careful." The next day he bought two large packages of potato chips, four super economy bags of cookies, five angel food cake mixes, 24 cans of Sprite....

The shelves in the cabinets are actually generous. They have to be. I told you before, when we left Virginia, we moved 57 cans of tuna fish and 38 cans of Vienna Sausage. This is the truth. I counted them.

K-Mart had my favorite brand of toilet tissue and paper towels on sale. I asked Hal to buy one large package of each. That was 24 rolls of toilet tissue and eight rolls of paper towels. He brought one of each into our condo on Tuesday. On Wednesday, he brought one of each into our condo. On Thursday, he brought one of each into our condo. I told him to stop--that he must take the last packages back to the car. There simply was no place left to put the paper supplies. We couldn't even get to the bathroom to use the toilet tissue.

He said he couldn't take them back to the car because it was full--of toilet tissue and paper towels. I told him he needs help.

FRIENDS???

Everyone has a "friend" who is perfect. Now, I don't mean just an acquaintance. I can deal with a flawless acquaintance as well as the next person--particularly if she's 20 years older or 30 years younger. I'm talking about an actual friend.

When you go into her home, you never see any clutter around. As you walk into her kitchen, you notice things are sitting around. For example, there may be a stack of books positioned in casual elegance. *This isn't clutter. This is planned--and it's intimidating*!

When you look around, there's no food that hasn't been put away. There's no spot on the counter that hasn't been cleaned. There's nothing in the sink. There isn't an overripe piece of fruit that insects are swarming around.

There's no opened loaf of bread on the counter. There are no unwashed pots on the stove unless dinner is underway--in which case, everything is neat, clean, organized and straight.

The candles are arranged flawlessly. In fact, they're burning when you enter. The shelves on the walls don't have any junk on them. There's no sign of something having been placed there to get it out of the way. No, everything on the shelves is put in a calculated position, just as they are on the coffee table and the corner of the room. The mirrors sparkle, the furniture is polished, and the carpet has just been vacuumed--even in the corners.

And then it occurred to me that I know where her weakness probably is. I've never heard her talk about dusting the shelves. They certainly are too high to be dusted without standing on a step ladder. I think about dashing home, getting ours, going back to my friend's home and inspecting her shelves. I bet there's dust on them! But, of course, I can't do that because it would embarrass her if there is, and me if there isn't.

This friend is a wonderful cook, too. She flaunts it. Actually, it doesn't take much to flaunt good cooking in my face since I don't especially like to do it.

You see, I, too, am a good cook and know that this comes as a shock to you. The reason I don't cook is because I don't want to make you feel bad because my cooking is so far superior to your cooking. Besides that, cooking really takes a lot of time.

But, back to my friend. There's never any dirt or smudge in her home.

The bathroom is so clean that you could eat right off the vanity counter top or out of the tub--either one.

In addition, her decorating scheme is perfect. She chose a theme and stuck with it. There was no anguish with her as to whether or not the wallpaper she picked was right, another picture was needed, if the border was a good idea or if an accessory was appropriate. Of course it was--or rather, they were. All of the above.

She's organized, too. She cleaned the house, wrote seven letters, addressed her Christmas Cards (it was only May), worked four volunteer hours, talked with three friends, surfed the net and had dinner on the table at 3:00.

I was exhausted and had to go home for a nap.

A DOUBLE S FORMATION

Six of us were meeting for lunch. Cindy and Kurt hadn't arrived yet, so we were standing around talking about one thing or another. The President and his latest affair surfaced-- of course. Surfaced in the conversation, I mean. Our friend said he didn't like the thrashing the President was getting by the Republicans. He said he had never known a Republican who wasn't rich, arrogant and self-righteous.

All throughout lunch we talked about that concept. During that day, and others following, the rich, arrogant and self-righteous people were on my mind. I decided that we needed to start a new organization for these folks. They, too, deserved a voice and an advocate. They deserved to stand tall and be counted. We would not demand that the members be rich.

We could call it the Arrogant Self-righteous group. Kurt suggested that we call it the Arrogant, Self-righteous Society. We could shorten it to an acronym of ASS. And so it was that the idea of the A Double S was conceived.

Now that the concept of the newest, greatest society had come about--and I was chosen to write the newsletter, I'm pleased to present the first newsletter from the new A Double S. I hope you'll enjoy it.

If you see yourself in this newsletter, if you would like to become a part and proclaim its principles to the ends of the earth, call me any time of the day or night. Just say that you, too, want to be united with those whose motives are of the purest, the noblest. Just say that you are willing to put your life on the line, and that you are ready to be a standard bearer and take a position for that which you believe.

If you have any questions about whether or not you qualify, talk with me. If you don't qualify at this moment, I'm sure we can help mold you so you will conform and fit in with the group. In the meantime, begin practicing the principles that are set forth in the newsletter. Remember, there are plenty of role models ready to take you under their wing and counsel you in the ways in which you should proceed.

You may want to belong to the parent organization only, or you may want to belong to the parent organization and all subgroups. Or any combination thereof. The decision is yours to make. There will be no judgmental analysis made of you. Everyone is good enough for A Double S--if you work hard to sear the principles into your soul. There will be no discrimination shown by the members.

I look forward to hearing from you soon.

A DOUBLE S NEWSLETTER

Volume One, Number 1

At its first meeting, the Charter Members of the newly formed *Arrogant, Self-righteous Society* (A Double S) elected its first President by unanimous vote.

In his opening remarks, the President admonished the group to be aware that having a name, a purpose, an organized group and a mission are meaningful only when each member embodies fully, embraces totally, and lives completely in accordance with the precepts and rules--which means that each member must live to his/her fullest potential to exemplify the true meaning of the organization.

Words will have purpose when actions are positive and supportive of all that the name says and implies. What each member does must speak so loudly that the words will simply be the icing on the cake. In other words, walk the talk.

The President elaborated on sub-chapters of the A Double S. He pointed out that while there will be a sub-chapter called PASS (Poor, Arrogant, Self-righteous Society), MASS (Moderate, Arrogant, Self-righteous), RASS (Rich, Arrogant, Self-righteous Society) and BASS (Bigoted, Arrogant, Self-righteous Society), he wanted to see the parent group firmly grounded with sound principles and purpose before placing his blessing on the sub-chapters.

The President pointed out that the group could become fragmented and the rich could be separated from the poor and/or the bigoted and that this would be detrimental to solidarity within the group and fulfillment of the principles of arrogance and self-righteousness upon which the organization was founded.

The President thanked the members for their confidence in him and promised to diligently pursue the purposes enumerated in the founding charter: (1) to foster fellowship, (2) to maintain dignity regardless of ridicule, (3) to hold oneself above others, (4) to know the high calling that enabled the founding and the foundation of the organization, (5) to remain in the world but not be a part of the world, (6) to promote arrogance and sense superiority--with humility--at all cost, (7) to remain humble at all times and (8) to realize that many are called but few are chosen.

He stressed that the organization would not be for everyone. There will be those who cannot meet and follow the standards primarily because their level of arrogance and self-righteousness are not high enough, but also because the physical appearance may not be suitable or income will not justify membership.

Language, nationality or race may also deter membership he said. In short, members must be well-dressed, have impeccable table manners, be at least fourth generation Americans and must use grammar that is commonly taught in the better schools--and above all must be arrogant and self-righteous--with humility. Whether they're rich, of moderate income or poor, the overriding concept will be an attitude of arrogance and self-righteous behavior.

The President said that he felt every man, woman and child could achieve the qualities required for membership if they would set their goals high and work to achieve them. It's truly an individual decision, but one not to be taken lightly.

The President stated that counselors were available 24 hours a day to help those who are not quite qualified to meet the rigid standards. He went on to say that no other organization could make that claim.

The meeting was closed with the President's thanking the group for maintaining a steady course and remaining faithful to the precepts on which the organization was founded, despite the difficulty in walking the narrow path that is more difficult than for a camel to go through the eye of the needle.

He stated that he perceived his primary job as President to be that of motivator, encourager and healer during difficult times.

The meetings are held daily at 9:30 a.m. and last two hours. Attendance is required for fellowship and networking. Members will want to negotiate business only with other members. If a suitable grocer can't be found, for example, members will simply have to do without food until a qualified person steps up to the plate.

The next program will be on the subject of "Bringing In More Sheep--And Feeding Them By Actions And Words--With Arrogance and Humility."

CHOCOLATE WITHDRAWAL

This morning I awoke to the clarion call of a charley horse in the calf muscle of my right leg, with the muscle cramp extending into my foot. Each muscle was screaming more than any other. I couldn't put my heel on the floor. It seemed as if it took 30 minutes to get my foot straightened out. The muscles in my leg and foot weren't the only ones screaming, today, yesterday and the day before. While exercise might be in order, I felt certain that a dietary supplement was needed.

It took this episode to make me take action to develop an exercise program with intent--one I would pursue diligently. Actually, I've had an exercise program for years. It had an agenda and a schedule. It was indelibly imprinted in my mind and, loosely translated, read something like this: perform the exercise that you want to, as much as you want to and as often as you want to. Well, there were times when I did want to, but it seemed that there were more times when I didn't than when I did. There was always tomorrow to exercise with intent.

This morning, though, I went for a walk. After a half mile, I couldn't take another step. Oh my, I hurt in places I didn't know I had. Hal was walking with me, and a half mile suited him even better than it suited me. We went in, had breakfast, and then it hit me.

These were chocolate withdrawal symptoms! I hadn't had a candy bar for three weeks. It wasn't that I didn't want one. It was mostly that Hal hadn't bought any when he went grocery shopping--which, you'll recall, is every day. True, Hal had brought Hostess Snowballs home. I ate all of them. They're chocolate. But, it wasn't the same. They don't satisfy the craving. They don't alleviate the muscle cramps.

Just to be certain that I had analyzed the medical condition properly, I reached for the phone to call my doctor. Our conversation would be enlightening because I could hear him say that I was right on target. The lack of chocolate could cause muscle spasms. That chocolate was absolutely harmless was a fact that needed to be proclaimed. In fact, the American population is chocolate deprived and should be adding chocolate supplements to their diet on a daily basis.

Further, the concept that breaking chocolate into small pieces, thereby releasing the calories so they can escape, is an absolute myth. Chocolate doesn't have any calories in the first place!

I was making notes on questions to ask and trying to leave enough space to write his answers. I wouldn't be able to record every word but I did make notes about the chocolate deficiency of most people who don't get enough chocolate in their normal diets and who should take supplemental tablets that are available in the form of *M & Ms* that will melt in your mouth, not in your hand. After all, if they melted in your hand, your body wouldn't benefit because the body can't absorb chocolate through the skin.

Since most people enjoy eating chocolate a good bit better than they enjoy broccoli, they could get the minimum daily requirement just from their every day foods by eating the right proportions of this basic food group.

I knew that I was doing great damage to my body by depriving it of chocolate. If the trend were to continue, the damage could be irreversible. It seems that the minimum daily requirement, depending on the weight of the individual, is two solid chocolate bars each day--such as a Hershey Bar with or without nuts--or six candy bars such as a Milky Way where there is less chocolate content.

In addition, weight gain from chocolate has been grossly exaggerated--particularly when the chocolate is consumed in its purest form. Chocolate is one of those rare foods that nutritionists have overlooked as an essential to good health and happiness. Besides all of that, chocolate helps to build strong bones because of the calcium.

Now, granted, I've paraphrased what I knew I would hear the doctor say.

These would not be his exact words. I've just taken the technical terms out and put the words into everyday language so that the average person on the street can understand the meaning of the conversation. That's the reason I feel comfortable passing it on to you.

Well, to tell the truth, the doctor wasn't in. But if he had been, and if we had discussed the subject, I feel certain that he would have said exactly what I've just told you.

WHAT'S WITH THIS PICKLE JAR?

Have you noticed how hard it is to open a jar of pickles? Or the ketchup bottle? Or to unscrew the top of the toilet bowl cleaner?

Have you noticed how a hand-held can opener just doesn't cut it any more (no pun intended)? I mean, it just won't turn. In case you haven't noticed, everything has been made difficult to open.

I won't even discuss the "child-proof" caps on bottles of medicine. But I will address the plastic wrapping on things. Even a box of candy is packaged as if it were part of an obstacle course, and the wrapping on a pound of bacon is enough to make you change your mind about breakfast.

But back to the pickle jar. It's not just that *I* can't open the jar. Hal can't open it, either. What sort of a vacuum pack is being used for packaging?

You see, we were sitting at the table trying to eat lunch. We decided to have hamburgers. We wanted a pickle. We were lusting for one--at least I was. The salivary glands were revved--in high gear, so to speak. It was a new jar of pickles. I tried to open it and failed.

I began again--and failed again. A gripping device was employed; still no success was realized. Do I need to tell you that I don't like to fail? I handed the jar to Hal--and asked him gentle, nicely and delicately to please open the pickle jar. He tried to unscrew the lid. He failed. He employed a gripping device and still failed. He doesn't like to fail, either.

He took the hammer and smashed the jar. "There," he said, "Now you can get your pickle."

How will he approach the bottle of toilet bowl cleaner?

EMAIL

Having discovered the delights of email, I find myself addicted to it (so what's new about me and addictions?). In the first place, it's so easy to do. Addressing an envelope and searching for a stamp seem to require too much effort. But, if you're going to do email, you must set it up right--even subscribe to various services--to guarantee that there will always be some whenever you check so you won't feel snubbed.

Some people never write a personal message on email; they just forward the thoughts of someone else. Often I'm pleased to receive them, or the jokes, or the poems, but it would also be nice if the sender were to say something like, "When I read the story about the ugliest fish in Dallas, it made me think of you, so here it is." That would personalize the story for me and would help me realize that the sender was a human instead of just a computer clicker.

Maybe a law could be passed to that effect. I mean, you wouldn't be able to forward anything unless you personalized it and took off the thirteen pages of addresses that show the origin of the email and the multitude of people to whom you're sending it. Somehow, the thrill of friendship is diminished when I realize that I'm just one of 78 people to whom you send everything that crosses your desk.

Can you remember the old days when you checked your mail and assumed the mail carrier hadn't been around because you had none? Remember how depressing that was? That never happens these days because there's always a fist full of junk. But, hey, if you didn't get junk mail, you might not get any mail at all except bills.

Well, just liken all of this to email. We couldn't count on having email each time we checked, so we subscribed to a free service. That led to at least 39 other free services, including several versions of lotto. Well--now we always have mail!

We know by the amount of email what our popularity level is--and we tell friends and anyone else who will listen to us just how much email we receive each day. After all, there's no point in receiving, if you can't tell about it. If our friends complain about the junk email, we're now in a position to join them. If they receive a good joke through email, they can forward it to us--or share it with us at dinner, just as we share with them. It's a new way to be an interesting, exciting person and to be the most popular kid on the Internet.

Just imagine receiving 41 messages in one day! Be still my heart. It's almost overwhelming. Whenever there's a lull in the conversation at a social gathering, just think of the ammunition we have to alleviate it and spark the life of others.

The possibility that some of it has merit and information that's valuable for these social occasions, not to mention one's work, is sufficient to send our blood pressure sky high. The amount of trivia alone is sufficient to fill our lives--and yours.

The reason for telling you all of this is to point out that this is an opportunity for you to take control of your destiny. If you want to have email, you have to arrange for it. If you want to learn interesting trivia from your email, you have to read it.

If you want to be an interesting group participant, you have to speak up and share what you know every chance you get. I didn't say discuss all of it every chance you get--just some.

Who knows, some of the minutia may help you when you appear on one of the quiz shows such as *Who Wants To Be a Millionaire?* Not that you'd remember the trivia at the time you needed it, not that your friend who knows everything would remember it, either, at the time when you used your "phone a friend" life line, but the audience would probably know it.

Regardless of whether or not an opportunity will ever exist for us to tell about our popularity or to use the bits of information we glean from this wonderful source, we feel popular, important and well-liked because there will be mail in the mail box when we check our email. It's refreshing and invigorating to us to realize that we probably receive more junk email than you do, and we know that whenever we check, there will be some kind of garbage there to enhance our sense of self-worth--and maybe once in awhile, there will be a note from a special friend.

CLOSET DOORS AND OTHER PHENOMENA

Our third bedroom has been transformed into an office/bedroom. It's a glorious room--by our standards--because it's multipurpose. It has 97 million linear feet of desk space, most of which is covered by computer monitors and printers. Ok, there's a bit of exaggeration in that statement. Nonetheless, the intriguing thing about the office is the closet door and the contents of the closet.

It was more important to have six file drawers--can you imagine that much file drawer space--than to have shelves for the printers. This was an either/or decision. We couldn't have both. This two member family is a multi-dimensional one with individual needs that include, but are not limited to, a computer and printer for each. But that isn't what I want to tell you about today.

I want to tell you about our closet. Well, actually, I want to tell you about all of them--but one at a time. The one I wish to talk about first truly seems to have unusual capability. You probably have a similar storage unit that has shelves, a rack for hanging and so on. Well, that's what ours has, too. No big surprises so far, are there? But, our closet has doors that are probably unlike the doors you have. This is the way they work.

I enter the room and close the closet doors. I turn around from my work and discover that they're open. I haven't touched them. So, I close them. Again, I do some work at my desk, turn around and notice that the closet doors are open. This goes on all day and part of the night I know for sure--maybe all night. I've never stayed up all night to determine that.

The last thing I do at night is close the closet doors. The first thing in the morning, they're open. Now, how would you explain these occurrences that appear to be connected with magic of some sort? And that's only one room. There are other remarkable doors.

In the guest room, I close the closet doors when I leave the room. When I re-enter, the doors are open. In the master bedroom, it's the same story. Not only that, though, a briefcase that's stored in the guest room closet jumps on the bed. So, you see, it isn't just the magic of doors. The magic seems to have been transferred to the things in the closet.

In the office, things jump out of the closet, also, but is isn't always the same item. In the guest bedroom, however, it's always the same item--the briefcase. In addition, the briefcase manages to spread its contents all over the bed. I just wish you could see it. You'd be as baffled by this phenomenon as I am.

Actually, our entire home seems to be possessed--or shall I say seems to be remarkable? It isn't only the closet doors and the contents of the closets that seem to be possessed with unusual powers. Wait until you hear about the drawers of the kitchen cabinets, the bathroom vanities, the desk and the dresser. They, too, have the magical power to open without any apparent assistance. The greatest mystery, however, is not the "opening;" it's the lack of a "closing" segment!

But you haven't seen anything until you watch the tube of toothpaste take it's cap off. It's almost obscene to view it in its semi-nudity. I mean, not only is it not fully dressed, but also the most important part is missing--and there's no telling what it may take off next. In public.

The final thing I'll mention to help you understand how it appears that our home may be possessed is the clothes hamper. It seems as if the hamper spews clothes onto the floor. This happens mostly in the evening--every evening--but sometimes during other times of the day, also. I mean, that's power. And to top it all off, it's only male clothes!

Have you ever heard before of such a situation as I've just described about the closet doors, drawers, the toothpaste cap and the clothes hamper? The reason I know there's magic involved is because Hal is as baffled as I am.

If this had happened one time or even two or three times, I might have thought that I left the closet doors open--or the drawers, or spilled the contents of the briefcase on the bed, or left the cap off of the toothpaste or dropped the clothes on the floor.

Perhaps this story should be sent to *Unsolved Mysteries*.

LOTTERY TICKET

Have I told you about my conservative nature? Please take my word for all of this. If you talk with Hal, you might get a distorted picture of this truth. My feeling is that anyone who eats peanut butter is thrifty. With this concept in mind--thrift that is--I told Hal that the only thing I wanted for Mother's Day was a lottery ticket. That seemed like a small thing to request. After all, it cost only one dollar. Well, actually, there was a bit more to the instructions. I told Hal I wanted the **winning** lottery ticket. I don't view that as unreasonable. It still cost only one dollar. It was a cheap Mother's Day gift.

The lottery that week was worth fifteen million dollars--not very much, but I'm not greedy. We knew we'd get only about fifty percent of that if we took a lump sum--about seven and a half million. Then Uncle Sam would claim his fifty percent. That would leave about three and a half--three and a half million dollars that is--give or take a little. While it's no great fortune, my needs are simple and it would do.

So, Hal bought a lottery ticket. A few days later he came running in, yelling for me. There are only three places where I ever am in our home--the computer, scrubbing or in the bathroom. Even though Hal says the last one commands more of my time than anything else, this time I was at the computer.

Anyway, he whipped out his lottery ticket and began spluttering. I urged him to calm down. He said he had won.

"Did we win the total amount?" I asked. I wanted details. In this case, don't start at the beginning. Just give me the bottom line if three and a half million dollars are at stake. Hal finally managed to get out of his mouth that he had won three and a half.

I was beside myself. I hugged and kissed him until he had to call for help to get me off. I had never seen three and a half million dollars all at one time before. Imagine! Where would it be put while we figured out how to spend it?

Suddenly, Hal seemed rather subdued about the entire thing and asked why I was getting so excited. Well-----, you've probably figured it out by now. My term of "three and a half" didn't mean the same as Hal's His was far more literal. He had won three dollars and fifty cents. That was a smidgeon different from what I had in mind.

There have been other times when we weren't on the same page, though they never involved as much money as this one did. Later in the day when I was calmer, I discussed this matter with Hal at length. Not that he responded at length, but that was the way I talked.

There are several basic principles involved here, and I don't want you to leave me without knowing just which ones I mean. To begin with, the same words can mean different things to different people. Secondly, even couples don't always think alike on issues. And third, if Hal had focused on the big picture of three and a half million dollars and had put that figure into his brain cells, he might have won that amount instead of three dollars and fifty cents.

PERFECTION

Have you ever fantasized that when you walk into a room, your regal bearing and extraordinary beauty will be so magnificent that all will be transformed by the very sight of you? You make your entry with your self-tan designed especially for your skin color--not too little, not too much. Your back is straight, tummy flat, abs perfect, no wrinkles on the face, no sagging arms, and a neck without blemish--despite the fact that you've never had a face lift. Your hair is casually cool--each strand as it should be. Not flat, not too poofy, a perfect length, streaked only by the kiss of the sun.

Your attire is without flaw. The color is *yours*! All parts of your ensemble are perfectly coordinated and assembled to reflect your inner beauty, impeccable taste and the fact that you know how to shop well.

All in the room would realize how you've risen above, and conquered, adversary--without whining or focusing on "poor little me." Your leadership qualities are as evident as your beauty and bearing. Your dependability and brilliance in being able to cut through the clutter of non-essential information to get to the important parts for decision making precede you.

The capability that you possess to discuss current events in any arena of interest, combined with your witty comments and infectious laugh make you a sought after guest for any and all occasions.

Your skills in home decorating and the maintenance thereof are without equal. Your home is the positive conversation of the town. Single handed, without benefit of a decorator or a housekeeper, though you could well afford both if you wished, you have created, and continue to maintain, a home of perfection.

House Beautiful has featured your landscaping, along with your home, and landscapers far and wide have visited to study the thought, focus and final result of your expert planning and execution of that which truly is a joy to behold.

Despite all of these accomplishments, you have remained unaffected by the adulation that follows you wherever you go, you have remained the same sweet, caring, compassionate, thoughtful and helpful person that you were before you created yourself.

With all of these thoughts swirling, you sleep--peacefully. You dream that you and your beloved are vacationing.

Suddenly, your elegantly casual attire turns into a pair of slacks that are stained and bleached--blemished from top to bottom. There's no way to hide the flaws, even in the dark.

As you're redressing, shamed by the fact that some may have seen you in less than a perfect state, you discover that your door is open and people are standing there talking, while you're hiding in a corner that you hope is not public. When they leave, you go to the door to peek outside and discover the brightness of the light is such that you can't see, you don't know where you are, your perfect love is not around--but a stranger is. You're in your partials--not fully dressed and coifed. The light will reveal any and all flaws.

The stranger tells you about the next construction project that will take place. He's talking about a building, but you believe he's using a parable to talk about changes that will happen within you--despite your perfection. There's no door to close. You've been exposed.

Oh, the pain, the realization that there may be a teeny, tiny flaw in your being. But where? If someone would only point out where you need to improve on yourself. "Freda, I don't have any clean underwear! Did you get gas? Do you plan to hog the Internet all day today? Did you make the appointment to have the air conditioner checked? When will the installers be here for shutters? Did you report the accident you had last night?" Did you find your keys? Where did you put my credit card that you borrowed because you couldn't find yours? Did you finish editing? How much money did your hypothetical investments lose yesterday?

ONE WAY STREETS

You probably use a map when you move to a new area--or even visit a place, unless you have an escort who's familiar with the city and takes you everywhere you want to go. I'm a map person and used one to learn how to get around St. Petersburg. In fact, in my wisdom, I took a high lighter and marked the route to my favorite places. I was so impressed with my genius that I gave a copy of the map, along with a written discussion of the directions (you didn't think I would miss the opportunity to use words, did you?) to others who were new to the area. Little did I know that many of the streets were one-way, and I had missed the name of the most important streets of all.

Our friend, told us early on that the avenues run east and west; the streets run north and south. Now, bear in mind that the streets are numbered--and so are the avenues--such as 1st Street, 2nd Street, 3rd Street and 1st Avenue, 2nd Avenue and so on. So, if I wanted an address that was at 2nd Street and 2nd Avenue, that was a piece of cake. But when I wanted to know the location of a store and someone told me it was at 4th and 38th, I still didn't know where to go. Was 4th the avenue--or the street?

As I pressed my informant, I sometimes realized which was which--but not always. Once I asked which came first--the street or the avenue. The person didn't even know what I was asking, let alone the answer. You see, if you've lived somewhere all of your life, you tend to know where you are and where you're going--and it's hard to identify with the person who doesn't know either.

In addition to the avenues and streets, the city is divided into north and south. And Northeast. That's with a capital letter.   Little, if anything, is said about "southwest" or "southeast"--just Northeast with a capital letter. In fact, it's Old Northeast. This was the first residential part of St. Petersburg to be settled. It's like a status symbol. You see, there's 10th Avenue North and there's 10th Avenue *Northeast.* Now that you think you're totally informed, let me help you a bit more. The downtown area of St. Petersburg has one way streets-- sometimes and in some places. For example, a street may be one way (like 4th Street and 2nd Avenue) for awhile and then two way for awhile. Or vice-versa, depending on the direction in which you're driving.

Since a person can't continue straight ahead, if the one- way direction isn't in his favor, he'll need to turn right--or left--to continue the journey. Sometimes a person could turn right and still be able to get to where he's going within a reasonable period of time, except that he can't do that either. He can only turn left--and he's in the right lane.

This presents a dilemma. The motorist who is in the right lane on a one way street and can't turn right and can't go straight might be beside herself--so to speak.

The drivers behind this unfortunate person don't know why she's indecisive. Soooo, they sometimes feel they can assist as she makes up her mind about her alternatives--of which there seem to be few, if any, and under the best of circumstances, fewer than hoped for. I've been motorist number one on occasion when helpful people from behind assisted me--by blowing their horns--an event that I find more than a little annoying.

Remember, we haven't lived here very long. In that short time, we've learned that there are many friendly people and many parades and/or times of celebration. It seems that there's a fireworks display almost every month. Consequently, when the horns sounded, I was startled but assumed it was a type of celebration. So I waved and began blowing my horn, too.

106

The only other alternative was to move forward, assuming the traffic allowed that. I didn't want to go forward. I wanted to turn right which, in this case, wasn't an option because the cross street was one way to my left.

Traffic was stopped dead still--in my lane. I didn't see any point in wasting gas, so I turned off my engine. I wasn't in a hurry and decided to join in the revelry. Well, actually, I was in a little bit of a hurry, but obviously I was in the middle of a happening, so I could either fume or join the fun.

Very privately I'll admit to you that I never purposely blow my horn at anyone or for any reason. Granted, the horn has been blown sometimes by accident, but never on purpose. My distinct preference is that others will not blow their horns at me. Still, this seemed to be a time of revelry.

There really was a lot of noise from the horns. I reflected on a time in history when a great noise caused a profound action. If you'll recall, the walls of Jericho tumbled when all of the trumpets sounded and the marchers shouted.

I don't know whether or not the motorists wanted anything to tumble on this particular day. However, buildings are being torn down every day, so I figured this might be one of those times when sounds, instead of dynamite were being used to level a building--and I was privileged to be a part of it.

As I said, I turned off my engine, opened the car door, got out of my car, closed the door, put the keys in my pocket, walked to the driver behind me and asked him what was being celebrated.

We've met a lot of friendly people here, but this wasn't one of them. He seemed to be really angry.

I don't remember all of his words, but he indicated I should move. He said I was in the wrong lane and the wrong street to turn right. I asked him if I should try to back up. He said I should endeavor to move forward, but those were not his exact words.

107

Further, he didn't seem at all interested in my destination--and even suggested another place where I could go, though I can't remember exactly where it was--oh, yes, I do remember.

I asked him if he'd like to get in front of me and help direct. I believe he indicated that alternative wouldn't be possible and that it would be best if I just moved forward and continued to muddle around, thereby getting out of the way--but again, those weren't his exact words.

Actually, I didn't hear much of what he said because it was so noisy. While I'm not the sharpest knife in the drawer, I got the impression that I was not in the middle of a celebration. Before we parted company, I mentioned to him that it appeared to me that he was experiencing a great deal of anger, and I was, too, because I just hate it when people honk.

To tell the truth, despite the fact that I had looked for a street sign for several blocks, one had not been found and I didn't know the name of the street I was on. The name of every cross-street--or rather, avenue was apparent because of the large overhead signs--5th Avenue, 4th Avenue, 3rd Avenue, 2nd Avenue. I even knew that I was in the North part of the city--not "Old Northeast" because I was in a business district.

And then I saw it. The street marker. "One Way." That was the name of the street! You see, previously I thought that was more of a directional sign rather than the name of a street.

Actually, it was the name of the next street and the next street. It was surprising how many streets had the same name. It seemed to me that several streets with the same name would be confusing to people who were unfamiliar with the city. Of course, on the other hand, it would be easier to remember the name of the street if every street had the same name.

Some people don't like the one-way streets. It's the business community that's the most vocal about it. If it will help the cause, I'll join them. Traffic doesn't move any better;

especially when the street is one way for a few blocks and then two way. Indeed, it didn't this day.

I was trying to get to the church but I couldn't turn where I wanted to. When I could, I did on "One Way" Street, which wasn't what I wanted and which necessitated circling the wagons for another thirty minutes before being able to make an appropriate turn on the desired street.

By the time I reached the church, it was needed more than when the trip started--and was probably also needed by the motorist who was in back of me. Well, to tell the truth, by the time I found the church, there wasn't anyone still meeting. In fact, the meeting wasn't even that day. It was the next day. As you probably suspect, this story isn't totally true, but it represents what I thought about doing when the man behind me sat on his horn and what I may do the next time if I have the courage. So, when I'm running late again and am stuck in traffic on a one-way street that doesn't have a name, you'd just better watch out.

EXERCISE AND FORGETFULNESS

Hal and I have tried various exercise programs--all with the best possible intentions. Somehow, we always falter after a few times at doing it. What we needed was a sure-fire type of exercise. In the course of time, because our memory is so bad, the non-fail system was revealed to us.

We always seem to need something that's at the other end of our home. If I was sitting at my desk, I needed a drink of water from the kitchen. So, I got up and walked to the kitchen. Upon my arrival, I turned on the TV, got the latest weather report and walked back to the office, sat down and began working at the computer.

It then occurred to me that I was still thirsty. I got up and walked to the kitchen, wiped off the counter, rinsed the sink, walked back to the office, sat down and began working at the computer.

My thirst level hadn't changed. I got up and walked to the kitchen. This routine was repeated for one reason or another many times during the course of the day. Every day.

It seemed that I walked miles just trying to figure out what I wanted or trying to find what had been misplaced. This led me to reflect on forgetfulness.

At six I remember, at ten I forget;
My brain's out for breakfast and isn't back yet.
It's not I'm forgetful, it's not I'm depressed;
I just can't remember; I'm not sure I'm dressed.

The food has all burned up; the heat was too high.
The grass hasn't been cut. The gas tank is dry.

111

The bills are not paid yet; do you know where they are?
Where's the book that I bought--do you think in the car?

I took memory courses to help me with names.
I'll think of yours shortly, but I'm not to blame.
Why don't you wear your name pinned up on your chest?
Then I can remember and give my brain rest.

I can't find my glasses, I can't find my keys,
I can't find my shoes, but I can find my knees
'cause they are attached, and I think that's the key.
But I'm not so sure that I'm really me.

BLUE TAPE

During our painting projects, a good bit of masking tape was needed. A person at the hardware store suggested blue masking tape as the ideal one to use. He said it would stick well during the project and could be easily removed after the painting was done. Blue tape wasn't one with which I was familiar--but I can assure you it sticks.

Of course, the exercise of choosing blue tape was easier said than done. In addition to all of the other colors of masking tape, there was, indeed, the eye-catching blue tape--in many widths--and it was considerably more expensive than the buff colored tape.

How could I justify paying three times as much for the blue tape? Regardless of the color, it would be thrown away after one use. And what width would I buy? Would it be preferable to get a wide tape for the ceiling or for the floor or for the corner?

One argument in favor of the blue tape was that it wouldn't be difficult to remember what sections had been "masked" so the paint wouldn't run into an area where it wasn't desired--which it might do anyway. My two concerns were whether or not it would stick when I wanted it to and remove easily when I wanted it to.

The tape did its job well. It stayed stuck on the wall, or wherever I put it, until the moment of removal. Because the color was bold, it was easy to determine where it was, and it kept the paint from running to undesired places. Doing a job well is commendable.

The tape came off the ceiling and baseboard easily--and, of course, it was disposable. Bear in mind, however, that while it was a disposable product, it developed a mind of its own and resisted. It didn't resist removal from the wall. Actually, that was the easiest part of the entire project--but after releasing itself from its original placement, it stuck to everything in sight. Trying to throw it away was a bigger effort than putting it on to begin with.

The tape stuck to me, my clothes, the newspapers and the plastic drop cloth that wasn't really cloth at all because it was plastic. Still, I was unprepared for the stick ability of this wondrous blue tape when I tried to put it into a plastic bag for disposal. It was clearly more of an effort to dispose of it than it was to mask the places where I didn't want the paint. It was, likewise, a humbling experience because I really didn't want anyone to know that I couldn't handle a piece of blue tape, put it where I wanted it and then throw it away.

On the other hand, the design the tape made on my clothes was rather striking, and if I were a clothes designer, it would probably have triggered an idea for the spring line.

Our neighbor stopped by as I fantasized about a new calling in clothing design while struggling to unwind myself-- which actually was an inopportune moment because the tape was wrapped around, on and above me, the plastic bag, and the step stool. She asked sweetly, "Where are you mailing yourself?"

TO SAVE OR NOT TO SAVE

There must be something to be said for saving money. You'll note I didn't say that I know what it is--just that there must be something to be said. By this time, however, you realize that I probably do have something to say on the subject--pro or con, or both. The long and short is, if you don't have it, don't spend it; if you do, do.

If you really want to know, there was a time in my life when that concept was very important. When I was in high school, for example, my friends would buy a milkshake--but I wouldn't because it cost $.20 back then. If I didn't buy it, I saved $.20. If I saved $.20 that day and many other days thereafter, I might have enough money to buy Christmas presents for family members--from my own money.

Probably the main reason I never became a smoker is because, a pack of cigarettes cost $.20--just like a milkshake. If I didn't have the $.20 for the milkshake, which I really liked, I certainly didn't have $.20 for the pack of cigarettes that I didn't yet crave.

This thought pattern didn't change when I went to college. My parents had apple trees. I didn't say that the apples were perfect. As a matter of fact, the trees were not sprayed, and the fruit was blemished. Despite that, I knew that a partially bad apple was also partially good. One bite of an apple was better than no bite of an apple. I was very fond of apples but didn't want to spend my money to buy them.

A peanut butter sandwich was sufficiently filling to take care of me at lunch and often at breakfast. It still does. This is one of my "I don't wanta grow up" foods because I still like peanut butter.

During my first two years in college, I ate a lot of faulty apples and peanut butter for breakfast and lunch and went with a roommate to the cafeteria at the university for dinner. The cafeteria always had mashed potatoes. Runny mashed potatoes. I didn't like them, but they were filling.

One thing I knew for sure was that if I ever had some money I didn't want any more watery mashed potatoes and gravy--or imperfect apples. While I won't tell you that mashed potatoes have never been served in our home, I will tell you that they don't run off the table--and for over 40 years, I didn't eat them. Or gravy.

Only recently have I been able to face having a mashed potato on my plate. Amazingly enough, when I finally decided to try mashed potatoes again, I decided that they're rather good when they are of the right consistency and served with a nice gravy.

At our home, I mash the potatoes and Hal makes the gravy. I would rather have potatoes that are almost as firm as a baked potato than to have them run off the plate. Lest you might think, however, that the potatoes are firm to the point of lumps, let me hasten to say that a lump wouldn't dare to show itself. This is not to imply that I'm a good cook or that I like to cook. Nothing could be farther from the truth. But I will state that we don't serve lumpy--or runny--potatoes.

As far as the peanut butter and the apples are concerned, you can mess with my diet in many respects, but don't mess with my peanut butter and apples. I like the chunky kind of peanut butter and am appalled at the lack of appreciation of some adults for the finer things in life. The cost is not important. The same with the apples. No more below standard apples for me. I want the nice kind.

Our friend introduced us to what may be the most expensive apple in North America--the Fugi. It's full bodied, firm, not too sweet, not too tart, doesn't tend to get overripe and mealy and can always be depended on to provide a

116

refreshing treat. Considering that I eat three or four apples every day, apples are a big part of our food budget. May I tell you at this point that a study has indicated that apples are "brain food" and may help with memory. Right now my memory says that the original subject of this discussion was not apples.

Hal realized early on that I was a cheap date. That's probably the reason he married me. I don't even drink coffee. The price of coffee is often not included in the meal when we eat out. Whatever the charge is, it's not worth it. How much does it cost to make a cup of coffee at home? A nickel? We've decided that if coffee or tea is not included in the price of the meal, neither will be ordered because two of one or the other will cost almost as much as the meal. That represents a luxury, and it isn't one of our choosing.

Actually, I didn't forego the coffee or the milkshake because I was *saving* money. I didn't buy either because each *cost* money, and I had so little of it. Money, that is. I was afraid I'd run out of that commodity.

I believe my four years in college cost $8.75. Ok, it was $493.12 more than that. I still have my expense record, and the small amount that things cost would blow your hair off--if you had any to blow.

When I go out to eat in a restaurant, my eye heads for the least expensive item on the menu. It's rare for me to deviate from that custom. Usually the most expensive items will be steak, prime rib, lobster or king crab. Because Hal likes red meat, we have more than enough of that on a daily basis at home and are very apt to have steak when we have company. I'm allergic to lobster and crab, so that leaves chicken and fish, which are usually less expensive than the others. So, again, I'm a cheap date. My cheapness saves us money--at that moment. I may spend it later on a luxury of my choosing--but not on food unless it's peanut butter and applies.

So, back to the first sentence. I'm good at saving money on food. I'm outstanding at saving money on furniture, accessories and clothes. I didn't say that little money is spent. I spend a lot because I'm good at it. One has an obligation to pursue that which she's good at doing. Since there are so few things at which I excel, I take every opportunity to revel in those I do.

If there's a bargain, I'll be the first in line. If an item is on sale, whether or not we need it, it must be bought. Still, I want to impress upon you that I'm a frugal, thrifty person--and if Hal should tell you otherwise, you should come back to me for further discussion.

The entire economy of the United States is dependent on people like me. You see, I buy consumer durables like clothes, bedspreads, paintings and accessories.

Hal buys consumer consumables like food. Hal is as good and persistent at his calling, which is shopping for food bargains, as I am in my calling, which is shopping for everything else. We probably have enough food in our home to last any couple for three and a half years. Hal said that everything was on sale--and he felt he had to buy multiples. By the same token, one might say that there are more clothes in our closets than are really needed. Lest you be so inclined to speak in that way, however, let me call your attention to the federal law about buying if it's on sale and you know it's on sale.

Once more, I'll reiterate the theme of this discussion--in case you've forgotten--of whether to save or not to save. I think that young people who don't have anything in the first place should save. I think that "seniors" who may or may not have anything at this point in life should take classes in how to spend more and more.

If they run out of money, they can eat peanut butter and apples.

MY FIRST HUSBAND

Hal is happier than he's ever been. Well, why wouldn't he be? He's been married to me for 46 years. The main reason he's so happy is because, after long last, I've finally gotten his thinking straightened out. Gently, yet deftly, he's been fed subliminal, positive thoughts about his unusually fortunate status in life. Now, I hear him saying the words that originally came out of my mouth. You see, Hal is my first husband--and I remind him of that daily.

It's taken many, many years and hasn't been easy. Some of lesser fortitude might have dropped out along the way. In fact, many did. Not "did" with Hal, but with their spouses. You see, Hal knows things about me that it's taken two lifetimes for him to learn. I don't share easily, so I doubt there will be a second husband--unless someone with documented enormous riches should knock on my door, completely smitten by my charm.

Hal says it isn't likely to happen.

I believe he meant the comment as a compliment--that no one else would have the courage to approach a person of my stature. Still, knowing Hal as I do, the comment might have the earmark of a double-entendre--or worse yet, a single-entendre (is there such a thing?) with a different meaning.

Oh, I don't think so. There's really no other meaning that could be ascribed to his comment because I treat Hal very well.

For example, when he does something right, I always compliment him. Well, ok, I haven't yet because he hasn't done anything right, but I'm prepared to do so just as soon as *he* does so.

119

Actually, he does some things right. One day he put the toilet seat down. But only because I told him that God wanted it that way or would have made sure that the seat was invented in the "up" position to begin with.

SHOE STRINGS

On occasion, people call Hal's attention to the fact that his shoe strings are not tied. He probably already knows it--especially when his foot slips out of his shoe. I used to wonder why he didn't tie them. You know, some teenagers don't tie their shoe strings, but usually Hal doesn't want to appear to be a teenager. Actually, it would be a little bit hard for him to do--to appear to be a teenager, that is--or to tie his shoes, either.

When the shoe strings are in bad shape and need to be replaced, the required length is hard to find. I used to keep extra pairs of shoe strings on hand. There were various lengths. My recollection is that they cost about $.25 per pair. Of course, that was when people wore a different kind of shoe, more like a dress shoe, that took a uniform shoe string.

Have you noticed how long the shoe strings are now for the typical sneaker type shoe that most people wear?

Well, it had been a long time since I bought shoe strings. I tried to buy a pair in a shoe store. They had the exact length Hal needed. They were $3.50. I nearly lost my balance. How could a pair of shoe strings cost $3.50?

It was right then and there that I told Hal he would have to keep his shoe strings tied because if he didn't, he ruined them, and they were too expensive to replace.

So, the next time we were out walking and I noticed that his shoe strings weren't tied, I asked him to stop and tie them. It was then that I learned why he hadn't tied them to begin with.

He couldn't.

He couldn't bend or stoop to tie his shoe strings.

I don't mean to imply that Hal is infirm. However if you should infer that I'm implying that his girth is such that it's difficult, or impossible, for him to reach his feet, you might be

121

right. If he's in a place where he can put his foot on something that's, say, two feet high, then he may be able to reach his feet.

For several years Hal has asked for assistance in removing his socks. Now, I thought he made such a request so he could be pampered. Maybe not. Maybe he can't reach his socks or tie his shoes. I'm not even sure he can *see his shoes!* Maybe the reason the slip-on type shoes are popular, or the ones with Velcro, is because many people can't reached their feet--for the same reason that Hal can't reach his feet.

Back to the day when I asked Hal to tie his shoe strings, and he couldn't do it. I knelt on the sidewalk and was tying his shoe strings--when a friend walked by. All of us said "hello." I didn't try to explain what I was doing or why--and the friend didn't ask.

Maybe he can't tie his shoes, either.

THE DRYER AND
RELATED THOUGHTS

The dryer had run for at least 45 minutes--maybe longer. Still, it hadn't given a signal that the clothes were about dry. Well, I guess it hadn't. When we returned from our walk, it was still going strong. I decided to turn it off because the clothes surely must be dry by this time. I always use the same setting.

Imagine my surprise when I realized that the clothes hadn't dried at all! Remember, we're talking about a dryer that's been used only about 12 months and already it isn't drying the clothes.

Examination of the controls revealed that a setting had been moved. I felt certain that it happened when I cleaned the front of the dryer--and inadvertently moved the control as I wiped the surface dry. Now, this is *not* to say that the dryer has been cleaned only once since the purchase date. It *is* to say that the moral to this story is *don't clean.*

The majority of frustration that a homemaker has is caused by things getting dirty and/or messed up after having been cleaned and straightened. Therefore, it follows, if you don't clean and/or straighten, you'll have fewer aggravations.

With that in mind, I plotted a course. There would be a re-allocation of time. The one and a half hours that Hal and I spent cleaning today would be spent another way next week. Think about it. We swept, scrubbed, vacuumed and dusted, collectively spending about three hours of our valuable time. We could have been doing other things.

For example, I could have taken a nap. Hal could have finished his book. I could have written three stories. Hal could have washed the car twice. Oh, oh, there we go cleaning again. No, Hal could have talked on the phone to someone--or several some ones. When the kitchen floor got dirty again, so what? It hadn't been scrubbed so who cares? When the dust settled again on the furniture--no big deal. It would just pile up on top of last week's dust. The papers and mail would be in disarray again, so any time and effort spent in organizing and straightening would be for naught.

And think about the bathrooms. Certainly those rooms are going to be soiled again. Now, I'll admit that cleaning might have to be done on occasion, but think about limiting it to, say, once or twice a year.

The only possible exception to the above decision to avoid cleaning would be clothes and linens. Still, I have a theory on that, too. For example, if the jeans, shorts, slacks and other outer wear stand on their own when thrown into the corner, you might want to consider washing them. As for undergarments, we all know the theory of wrong-side out. Maybe upside down would also work.

All I'm saying is that you would not only save money on cleaning products, you would save electricity from running the washer and dryer less often, and just think about all of the water that could be saved. Valuable time could be spent doing something worthwhile like watching the shopping channels on TV. Or you could join a chat room on the computer.

In the event that you're a compulsive, you could at least work out a cleaning schedule that is less frequent. To illustrate, instead of cleaning once a quarter, you could reduce the cleaning by one-half or three-quarters.

Women of the world, I'll guarantee you that your husband and children will never know the difference in the appearance of your home. The only thing they would notice would be a reprieve from sharing responsibilities.

And think of the stress and wear and tear on your nervous system that would be saved. You might live several years longer to look at your dirty home if you were to follow these few suggestions.

If God had meant for you to have a clean house, she would have provided a free full-time maid to every family.

NEW FLATWARE

We went to Sam's Club--the big store that has everything where you must pay a membership fee to shop. As soon as a branch near us (is 25 miles near?) opened, Hal talked about visiting the store to determine if the prices justified the trip and the annual fee. I knew that when we went into the store that all of the criteria would be met--in Hal's opinion. I didn't realize that I would make the first purchase.

The main problem with such a store as this is that there is so much to tempt the weak person. For example, there are a wide variety of grocery items. However, there are also clothes, books, tires, televisions and related items, hardware, office supplies and silk flower arrangements. A shopper might have been happy without some of these things if he were not in a store where those items were. But to be tempted by that variety each time he shopped for groceries might be more than the temptation level can handle.

For example, items are packaged in large units. A woman was giving away free samples of breakfast pizza. It was pleasing to the taste, so Hal picked up a package of it. It just happened that the package was the big, industrial size. It was almost two inches in depth and at least 14" square. "Where will you put that box in our freezer?" I asked.

"The lady mentioned the box could be opened and individual pieces taken out and stored on the shelves of the freezer door."

"Ok, Hal, what's presently stored on the shelves of the freezer door?" I asked.

"I don't know. Ok, I'll put it back."

He did--because I was with him. If I hadn't been along on this trip, he wouldn't have put it back.

We came to a shelf that had spray starch. I use some on the crease of the sleeve of Hal's shirts. I made the mistake of mentioning that I needed a can. Hal picked up the package.

"Hal," I said, "there were 10 cans strapped together. One can lasts me over a year. Can you see me struggling to find space for 10 cans for the next 10 years?" He put the package back on the shelf.

As I said previously, I'm not immune to "monkey see, monkey buy" either. I saw a package of flatware, with 12 place settings plus serving pieces. The pattern was pleasing, and the labeling said it was heavy quality stainless steel. Have you had stainless steel that was so flimsy you bent the knife and fork when you cut through a hamburger?

The price was as pleasing as the pattern. My heart was going pitty pat very rapidly at this point. Our present flatware was originally for 8. There hadn't been 8 of anything for a long time. Normally we don't have more than 6 guests for dinner at a time, but even then, a place setting for 8 with a few pieces missing just won't cut it unless the dishes were washed just minutes before the arrival of guests and between courses.

The possibility of having 12 pieces all from the same set of a respectable weight stainless was almost more than I could bear. Needless to say, the thought had crossed my mind before, but here, at this very moment, the price was right.

By the time I met up with Hal at a designated time and place in the store, I had drooled all over the box. I *had* to take it now. Hal thought it would be all right. Why wouldn't he? He wasn't the one who would have to find a place to put the old flatware. Surely, you didn't think I would give it away, did you? I might need it sometime--when we have 18 or 20 people for dinner.

The first thing I did when we got home was to unpack and wash the new delight. It was magnificent! Before it could be put in the drawer, however, the old had to be washed (I didn't want any stray pieces left in the dishwasher and mixed with the new) and packaged for storage. And, of course, the tray in which the new would be placed had to be washed.

When the new flatware, all 12 pieces of each size, was put into the flatware tray, it was a joy to behold. Be still my heart! I wouldn't have to contemplate whether or not company was coming tonight--or tomorrow before the dishes were washed. It was almost more happiness than I could handle to look at 12 of each in one drawer.

I visited the flatware drawer several times that day--and the next and the next. It takes so little to turn me on.

THE JUICY POTATOES

Ok, you already know that Hal likes to shop, likes to shop often, likes to buy anything and everything he sees and has been known to buy more than he should. Just imagine for a moment that Hal bought potatoes on Monday, then he bought potatoes again on Tuesday, again on Wednesday, and as a result, there was an abundant supply of potatoes on hand. That many potatoes couldn't be eaten fast enough to avoid spoilage. And then the next week, he repeated the procedure, forgetting that he had bought potatoes--several times-- the previous week.

Of course, there are several different types of potatoes. Red Potatoes are good for boiling or for mashing. Idaho potatoes are especially good for baking. Having a supply of "mashing" potatoes on hand might not suffice if one were having guests and wanted "baking" potatoes or vice versa.

Out of sight, out of mind is a concept that Hal and I deal with constantly. We're both visual people. If we don't see it, we don't think about it. That applies to paying bills, reading the newspaper, serving watermelon and everything else. Because of this, almost everything we own is on the dining room table or the kitchen counter--or the top of the desk.

Hal likes to have the tomatoes on the counter. He says they aren't as good when put in the refrigerator before eating them. Frankly, I can't tell any difference. Nonetheless, I humor him by leaving the tomatoes in a container on the counter.

The counter, while spacious, wasn't designed for storing all of the food items. Cabinets were designed for that--as was the refrigerator. When the refrigerator is full, one must resort to storing foods on the cabinet shelves. I learned long ago not to store potatoes under the sink because of the heat from hot water going down the pipes. Previous to that bit of knowledge, I thought there was a federal law that specified the cabinet under the sink as the only place allowed--but I was wrong.

Because our refrigerator is always full and running over, I put the potatoes on a shelf in the cabinet. As it turned out, I didn't have all of them together. Some of them were in the refrigerator. Again, out of sight, out of mind.

Remember the new stainless steel flatware with 12 place settings? When that was put into the appropriate drawer, the old had to be put somewhere else. I opened a cabinet to do just that and thought the cabinet had sprung a leak! There was liquid coming out of it. My first impulse was to close the door and run--so I did.

Realizing that I might as well determine how the cabinet could miraculously be a source of liquid, I opened the door again. This time I remembered one of the reasons I closed the door quickly on the first round. I was met by an odor that I couldn't identify. It definitely was not perfume!

I closed the door again but then realized the source of the odor should be determined.

Research revealed that this was the cabinet in which the potatoes were stored. Some of the potatoes had gotten, shall we say, "ripe." In fact, they were past ripe. This state of over ripeness was causing the leak as well as the odor.

This was not my first experience with ripe potatoes. Still, I don't ever remember potatoes having so much juice! Only two or three of the potatoes were overly ripe. However, there was enough juice for potato soup. *How could the potatoes have so much juice?* If you were to put potatoes in a pan to cook without any oil or water, there certainly wouldn't be this much juice!

It took a bit of doing, but all of the juice was finally cleaned up, the refrigerator was checked for potatoes, and the entire lot was rewashed, dried and put into the refrigerator.

Of course, that meant that a refrigerator bin had to be washed. If it was washed, the shelves might as well be washed. And the door. But not the other bin. Well, ok, wash the other bin, too.

Have you noticed how a simple pleasure like new stainless flatware can balloon into an afternoon's work?

CLOTHES THAT BIND

It was time--way past time--to evaluate the situation. Not only was more room needed, but there was also no point in continuing to try to delude myself into thinking that I could ever get into some of those clothes again. The clothes that went around last summer, did so grudgingly. The resulting appearance, after the skirt went around, was sufficiently grotesque that I wouldn't be seen in public with it on. Mixed with the remarks of despair about trying to fit around an object larger than the clothing item, were chuckles that were audible two floors above me. Not me--I wasn't doing the groaning and laughing--it was the clothes that were having such a blast.

Granted, it would have been difficult to carry on a conversation when wearing these items because I couldn't breathe, and the clothes didn't enhance my figure in any way. Instead, they seem to work very hard at pointing out every flaw. Still they didn't have to exhibit such rude behavior.

In the past, I've used a jacket to hide a skirt waistband that refused to button. At this point, the situation had advanced beyond that stage

This was going to be a difficult day. Parting with my beloved clothes had never been easy in the past. Yes, as you've already figured out, this isn't the first time the closet had to be purged. You see, I don't buy many clothes that I don't like. The few items that were in the closet that I didn't like were easy to part with. That would be the place to start.

However, most of the clothes are my absolute favorite. One of the reason I've held on to them this long is that I really like them. Another reason is that its difficult to part with clothes that have been useless for less than ten years.

So it was with much weeping and wailing that I began to pull out those items that simply wouldn't stretch comfortably or attractively, with or without a jacket. Some of the anguish was caused by the fact that there wouldn't be anything left to wear. Well, not that I was wearing them anyway--because, as you'll recall, they didn't look good and I couldn't breathe in them. Still, an empty closet is an unsettling thing--not the kind of situation that I enjoyed creating.

I already know the bright side of this picture. This was a shopping opportunity. I knew in my heart, though, that there would never be another royal blue pleated skirt as magnificent as the one that was leaving me. There would never be another match for my emerald green jacket that was as spectacular as the skirt that was no longer comfortable.

To add insult to injury, the printed skirt that was so devastatingly smashing with the emerald green jacket had an elastic waistband. All around. Without the jacket, I looked like the *Goodyear Blimp* in it. Nonetheless, I loved it and parting was not sweet sorrow.

Almost as disturbing as the departure of the skirts is the fact that the jackets still fit. Does that tell you something?

Have you ever noticed that women who are well-endowed between the neck and waist become more so as the years pass while those who weren't, don't? You would think that in all fairness, just the opposite would happen. Aside from that, what skirts would I wear those wonderful jackets with now?

I gently and lovingly took each item of clothing that was no longer suitable to wear and hung it one place or another on an over-the-door hanger. That way, I could continue to gaze longingly at that which was important to me in another life.

There were some items that I hadn't seen since we moved. You see, the closet, while generous, was "organized" by yours truly to function efficiently. That means skirts were put on skirt hangers that are 4 to 6 skirts tall. A skirt that was hung on the second rung from the top--or the bottom--might never be seen again in this life.

Now, the skirts were hung over the door in one room, the slacks on still another door and the shorts on another. They looked more beautiful and splendid than ever before. How could I part with them?

The pair of lined, white linen slacks, bought when I lost a few pounds twelve years ago and were wrinkled before I got to where I was going, looked splendid. The wool slacks, bought when a store was closing and had reduced the price to a ridiculously low level looked resplendent on the hangar. They, too, were bought during one of my "skinny" periods. Of course, they were also bought when we lived where wool slacks felt good during the winter. Sweaters were purchased to compliment the color and style of the slacks.

The shorts that had been taken out of the closet were also a joy to behold. I could actually still button some of them and breathe--if I was standing up and didn't eat. I had dressy blouses, casual shirts and even more casual knit tops that matched the skirts, slacks and shorts perfectly. Oh, my heart was aching!

If I were to walk two miles every day, use the ab industrial strength steam roller ten minutes every day, refrain from all chocolate for the rest of my life, I could lose five pounds. Five pounds might not allow me to get into all of the clothes. It might take ten pounds.

Could I do it? All I needed was the motivation of the agony of parting with my beloved clothes. No, it would last only for a few weeks--or days.

I took one last loving look at the clothes, so neatly organized on hangars. I caressed them, and spoke gently to them.

Then I took the hangars, put them back in the closet, quickly slammed the door and ran out of the condo.

That was a close one!

CONTAINERS AND PACKAGING

Do you ever notice how products are packaged? You know that many things are wrapped two and three times. For example, microwave popcorn comes in a bag that can be put into the microwave. Then there's a plastic bag around that bag. Then a box with several plastic bags put into still another box, with plastic covering the entire thing. The dilemma is what to do with the outer stuff. In the case of popcorn, I know to throw it away; but read on about other types of containers of which it's harder to dispose.

One product that is packaged only twice is the individual tablets that are made for use in the dishwasher to replace loose powder. They're minutely less messy than the powdered products. It's probably true that the "tabs" cost more than the loose powder--but we decided to try them anyway. The brand that first came to our attention packed its 26 "tabs" individually and then put them into a tubular cardboard container that looked much like the ones in which tennis balls are bundled.

It's true that the ease in using this new and improved product is special--not that it took very long to use the powdered type of detergent, either. A repairman told us to load the detergent dispensers before the clean dishes are taken out. That way, the cups don't get water In them and cause the detergent to cake--and not dispense properly. There are two detergent cups to be filled, and we always did fill them when we used the loose power products. Now, tell me, how does one detergent tab in one cup do the dual job that two cups of the loose powder did? That isn't the issue that's being addressed here, however. It's just something for you to think about. It's the container that fascinates me.

139

The sturdy cardboard container with a lid can probably be recycled for any number of craft projects just as soon as the creative crafter gets her hands on it. In the meantime, what am I to do with it? We have a collection of these already. Indeed, the container is much too nice to throw away.

This dilemma reminded me of my early days. My mother didn't throw away a piece of string, or a rubber band--or anything else and neither do I. Well, I became my mother when I was 8. I saved every little thing as much as she did. If a straight pin came in a new shirt, the pin was saved. If a paperclip came with a piece of paper, it was saved.

Actually, I don't have any problem with packaging of, say, a man's shirt.

Well, maybe I do because there are so many separate parts, but I understand the outside plastic bag, the 48 pins used to pin the shirt as it's folded at the factory; the stiff cardboard under the back collar to provide support and prevent wrinkling so the shirt looks good when it's displayed in a store; and I understand the piece of clear plastic that's used at the top button of the folded, buttoned shirt. I also know now that the pins are not good ones to save for sewing projects, so I throw them away--along with all of the other packing pieces except the cardboard which I may need someday to stiffen a package when I mail a valuable document.

The oblong, heavy cardboard container in which the dishwashing detergent tabs are packed is another thing. I told you this is a sturdy, well made container. But not waterproof. So how can it be recycled?

I understand what to do with the plastic jar with a screw on lid that the peanut butter comes in. Save it! I might use the jar for left over gravy, or the grease from cooking hamburgers so either one can be disposed of without messing up the entire world. Or, I might use the jar to store left over paint.

I understand what to do with the packaging around microwave popcorn; throw it away. I understand what to do with the vacuum wrap that surrounds a pound of bacon; throw it away. I understand what to do with the band that acts as a second sealer for the container of cookies; throw it away.

I still don't know what to do with the tennis ball type container in which the detergent tabs were packed, of which I now have six.

What would happen if I threw it away?

THE NOSE

The Nose is with me--always, even until the end. It makes its presence and needs known at meetings, social events, in the mall, the office--and the most annoying time at all--at the dinner table. There seems to be no end to the attention it must draw to itself. Its Majesty has chosen to be allergic to everything, everywhere, 'til the last trumpet sounds, and I fear it will drive me out of my office.

It seems that warm foods are sufficient to trigger The Nose, or cold foods, or a combination of hot and cold, which, incidentally, is sufficient to set off a reaction of which a volcano would be envious.

A wind is sufficient to set it off--or the lack thereof. A dry room will trigger The Nose--or a humid room or a perfect room.

The Nose cannot tolerate feathers or fresh flowers and will make a real production about perfumes of any type, shape or description. The Nose cannot tolerate spices or newspaper print. If you really want to know, The Nose is not an adaptable object.

It cannot "take it or leave it" as some other things in life can, and is rarely, if ever, neutral. It's not objective; rather, it has an opinion and has no reluctance in letting the sentiments be known. Since removing The Nose is not an alternative, the owner--that would be me--has had to learn to live with it.

The Nose is either stuffy--to one extent or another--making normal breathing uncomfortable--to one degree or another--or runs. There are a few precious moments when the greatest of my challenges is neutral. If you should ever encounter such a time, savor the moment. It won't last long, it might not happen again soon, and it definitely won't happen often.

Perhaps the most unsettling thing The Nose has done recently is to carry on big time as soon as the owner enters the office. There are sneezing, drippy, blowing bouts--and there simply is no end to it. Since the owner of The Nose wears no perfumed products and allows no one with perfumed products into her home, she wonders what is happening. Since a fair amount of printing activity takes place in that room, since there may be paper dust in that room, and since newspapers are sometimes carried into that room, there is a chance that any one, or a combination thereof, may be the culprit.

Just in case you aren't understanding the full significance of my statement about The Nose and office, please remember that many of the waking hours of the owner of The Nose are spent in this location. It's the shrine, the sanctuary, the work place, the escape, the Shangri-la.

In the office, there are no feather pillows, no silk flowers, no live plants, no detergent, no hand lotion, no after shave and no spices. Despite all of the thou shalt nots, so to speak, there *is* something to which The Nose responds. In a big way.

As soon as the printer gets into high gear, The Nose does, too. But, even when the printer is in low gear, or no gear at all, The Nose is still in high gear.

It's in gear in the morning, in the evening, in the in-between time and a combination of all of the above. Since newsprint is such a culprit and seems to set the pace for the day, beginning at the breakfast table, is it possible that newsprint is still on my hands when I go into the office? And then, when the printer begins, do the ink and the paper combine to irritate The Nose? Or is it seasonal?

Think, for a moment about an X-ray technician and the procedure she uses to perform an X-ray on you. She/he gets everything lined up and then steps out of the room while the machine does its thing. Do you suppose the owner of The Nose will have to do that, too? Step out of the room while the printer works? I can see it now. Click on "Print," jump up, run out of the office, close the door, take a walk while the printer performs, and then return to the office when it's all over--just to repeat this joyful experience every time a page is printed.

The good news is that *I do have a nose--and have only one*. Just imagine if you didn't have a nose--or if you had two of them?

The Nose is with me always. Even until the end.

I FAILED KOFFEE KLATCH *101*

This is serious. How can I ever break into polite society, or be accepted into the community and avoid being an outcast. I failed Koffee Klatch 101. A long time ago.

We were in a new community, many couples were about the same age as Hal and I and many had children the same ages as ours. Some of the young mothers liked to get together around mid morning--for coffee. I don't even like coffee--and I didn't have the time. How did the other women have time to drop everything to go have coffee?

In the first place, the baby's diaper had to be changed and his snowsuit put on. The oldest child could get into his own snowsuit, but couldn't handle the boots. The middle child wasn't old enough to do anything for himself yet. So, after they were dressed, I had to put my coat and boots on to walk across the street to the neighbor's house. As soon as the door was locked, the middle child had to go potty--real bad that instant!

Take stuff off, potty, put stuff back on, walk across the street, take the children's stuff off--including the boots, find a place to put them where I would be able to find them later and know they were our boots. With the speed of lightning, they managed to get into something they shouldn't and began fighting with each other or the other children.

"Mom, Billy hit me."

"Mom, Michael said a bad word."

"Mom, can we go home?"

The neighbor would also have a "coffee cake" which she had made from scratch and which would be a gourmet delight. My turn to be hostess would come soon. What "delight" would

I concoct--and when? What could I do to avoid failure? With three children under five years of age, it was not going to be my cup of tea--coffee.

Of course, if I didn't go, I could be the subject of conversation because some might think I was snooty. As a minimum, the other women would form a bond that would exclude me.

Somehow, it seemed, that I just didn't fit in with the other women. Some of them were already on a bowling team, some spent all day at the pool in the summer. Here I was, I didn't even drink coffee and certainly didn't have the time or energy for bowling--or the money. Besides that, I didn't swim or hang around the pool for hours of sun bathing.

This was not a totally new situation for me. Even as a child, there were others who did things that were totally uninteresting to me--or if they were interesting, my mother had sufficient projects for me to do to prevent my interfacing with the unimportant and/or mischievous things that she assumed other children did with their time.

Even during college days, I didn't enjoy spending hours playing cards or sun bathing. I mean, yes, some of each was ok, but all afternoon, day after day?

Not fitting in was almost a pre-set pattern for me, it appeared. You see, I've always been a project person. I like to see something at the end of the day that I've accomplished. Well, not that I ever did with three young children, unless you consider washing diapers (which we did do in those days), cleaning food off of the faces of children and the ceiling, and putting the tomatoes back on the shelf where they were ripening before the neighbor's children (and ours) decided to use them for bowling balls--as completed projects. Somehow, these "projects" never seemed to interest Hal too much.

Still, failing Koffee Klatch 101 would be an embarrassment that might follow me all of my days. To get right to the bottom line, I did and it has. I'm still not part of the gang. Even when I'm part of the gang, I'm not part of the gang.

Well, ok, it's time for the truth. I know how to turn on the oven to bake a coffee cake, but my recipes didn't seem to turn out to be as spectacular as those in the Koffee Klatch--and besides it took and takes so much time to do it. I could and can buy one already made, warm it in the microwave, but the others still did and do their gourmet thing--and I'm still failing Koffee Klatch.

WHERE DOES THE SLEEP GO?

Why is it the minute I put my head on the pillow to go to sleep for the night that my mind starts pouring out thoughts? The words flow, tumbling over each other as if in a rampage. There are enough words rampaging to make a whole book and/or to provide material for a stand-up comedian.

Never mind I may so sleepy that I dozed while watching my favorite TV program and dropped the remote control. Never mind that I slept for 35 minutes in an awkward position. Just as soon as I put my head on the pillow, that's it. No more sleep for me. Just thoughts.

The thoughts that flow, tumbling over each other as if in a rampage are funny. I amuse myself so much that I'm apt to be awake for three or four days. It's the emphasis on the words that's so funny. I can see myself, a stand-up comedian, making people laugh so hard that they fall off their chairs. Why do they laugh? Because they've been there. The same thing has happened to them, and I'm telling them what they already know. I emphasize certain words. It's as if the audience has never heard the words before. Especially in the combination I'm using.

It definitely isn't as if no one else has ever had the experience being described. If so, the experience wouldn't be funny. What would be funny if I told you I rode in a hot air balloon while eating an ice cream sundae upside down? There's nothing funny about that. No one has ever done it. In the middle of the night or any other time. Ok, it's impossible, but that has nothing to do with it. It just isn't funny.

But when I'm a stand up comedian, and I tell my audience that when I put my head on my pillow and I can't sleep because my thoughts flow, tumbling over each other as if in a rampage, that's funny because you've experienced the same thing, and you probably thought you, too, could be a stand-up comedian and punctuate those words just as I did except you didn't do it, and I did. *Be a stand-up comedian. What did you think I was talking about?* I was a stand-up comedian for that moment, at least. In my fantasy.

Please pay attention so you'll know what I'm talking about and what's going on. Now, I've forgotten what I was going to say and a good stand-up comedian can't do that. Granted she can pause for laughter and that might give her a chance to reorganize her thoughts. But not much.

What else would a comedian reorganize except thoughts?

To be perfectly honest with you, I wrote an entire book and a comedy routine that would last a year--last night when I couldn't sleep--that is, I wrote it in my head. The reason I didn't get up and write all of the words down was because that would have really made me wide awake. I thought if I stayed very still I would fall asleep in a few minutes. Wrong!

Those words are probably lost forever. Do you suppose they went to word heaven? Maybe God didn't want me to use those words--if she did, she'd help me to remember them now. Oh, my, they were funny. I was practically rolling off the bed laughing.

Well, next time I'll get up and write the words down. Or else I'll do laundry.

ME AND THE COMPUTER

Some interesting things have happened on the way to the forum--that is, on the way to using the computer in a heavy duty way. The computer became disabled on numerous occasions. There was no alternative except to turn it off and begin again. I don't know what it was thinking, but I do know that no matter what I told it, it balked and sometimes flat out wouldn't respond at all. Despite the cantankerous nature of it, I was finally able to accomplish my purpose until one fatal day when I lost Word Perfect from my computer. I didn't lose my disc, just Word Perfect. Totally and completely, Word Perfect was gone.

However, whether or not I lost my work became a moot point if I couldn't get on my computer to view and edit. The version of Word Perfect that I was using was an old one-- the one on which I first learned to use the computer.

You see, I was speedy on my original word processor that pre-dated Adam and Eve. It was reliable, I could save, correct and print. Granted, the printing was slow and the page was beaten to death by the strike of the keys; nonetheless, it did the job--and I knew how to use it. When I began to use the computer, I nearly had a total collapse. I felt as if life, as I knew it, was over and I would never be proficient again. As much as I hate that I'm resistant to change, it became apparent that such was the case.

Never mind that deep inside I knew the computer would be faster in the long run, that the capability was greater and that my creativity (assuming there was some) could be used to the max, the underlying fact that it would take time to learn the computer and I would be slowed down for a while always took precedence over any other realization. So I procrastinated until I was embarrassed to be around my computer literate friends--many who were much older than I.

So, now, having taken the plunge to learn a word processing program on the computer--one that would even allow me to illustrate brochures--it would take time to readjust to another program.

I had been spending my time in two ways. As you surely must realize, there's this book that I'm intent on writing and I was doing day trading for which I don't want a lecture and anyway, it's not what we're talking about today.

Do you remember when I told you about the fast clicking and One Command at a time? I don't just make up these things. They really happen to me. Well, as I just told you, after experiencing the agony of learning how to use the computer, it crashed. This wasn't the first time, but it was the most complete crash. Apparently, I clicked too fast and gave too many commands at a time. The computer told me in no uncertain terms from time to time about the despicable things I was doing. I felt like a schoolboy who specializes in misbehaving. But this one day, it gave no warning and just bit the dust and took Word Perfect with it.

Well, I was out of business. Oh, You Tee--out. Hal was by my side. He called computer stores trying to find the same Word Perfect program that we lost. No store had it. Finally, he dragged out his old computer which he felt was unfit for his meager needs and was now stored in a closet, bought another keyboard and mouse and connected it at my desk.

There's more to this than meets the eye. You see, our desk is custom built, and cords run through specific openings-- and the printer had to be connected to computer number two that was at my desk, along with computer number one.

Using a different keyboard meant making an adjustment. Fortunately, my patience survived the test, and the diskettes on which my "book" had been saved allowed me to begin editing. And to continue writing.

In the meantime, Hal continued to search for the old Word Perfect software so he could reload it on computer number one. He was triumphant, which means that there were now two functioning computers at my desk, plus a computer at his desk, which I'll fondly call "computer number three."

So, the time came when I worked for a few minutes on computer number one--I can't remember now why. Maybe it was to save my newly written and edited stories on the C Drive of computer number one. And so it was that I found what I perceived to be the right mouse, the right "tower" for the computer, and began giving commands. Oh, joy of joys, it didn't crash. However, it didn't save, either.

I wanted to change the name of a file, typed the new name--and nothing happened. Computer one wouldn't change from one name to another. In frustration, I shut the computer down, got the mouse in position for computer two--and then realized I was using the keyboard for computer two when trying to give commands to computer one.

The pressure was on. I hadn't made my quota for the week. I was ahead on Wednesday, but Thursday wasn't a good day, so I was now behind on this Friday. It was very stressful. In addition to the quota, I was now using three computers. Yes, I used Hal's part of the day and two at my desk. I was using the mouse for one, the keyboard for another and the monitor to something.

You probably don't have situations like this. And you see, that's how I get behind and don't make my quotas and feel pressure.

SHRINKING AND DISINTEGRATING

You know that you have to clean the lint trap in the clothes dryer after each load of clothes has been dried. You know how much lint is in the trap--and you know that a good crafter could find a use for the lint. In the first place, the birds would be greatly pleased to have the lint for their nests. My question is, is the dryer gaining as much weight by eating my clothes as I appear to be because my clothes are being eaten by the dryer as it shrinks and disintegrates them.

It isn't just the lint trap, however, that collects lint. Have you ever examined the exhaust from the main pipe of the clothes dryer? You may have something over the opening to catch the lint--like a piece of ladies nylon hosiery. There's a lot of lint that comes out of that pipe!

So you see, it may be that you haven't gained weight at all. It may be your clothes are disintegrating--in the girth area. And if so in that area, that same disintegration would also affect the length proportion, also. Therefore, instead of contemplating the next diet plan, maybe you could curse the clothes dryer instead. As a minimum, it might make you feel better to acknowledge that the reason your slacks are tight is because the dryer is eating them and then spitting them out--rather than the fact that you've gained weight--again.

Having said all of this, the question arises about why the dryer would eat the clothes in the first place and why it would, after having had its fill, regurgitate some of it into the lint trap and still more into the exit tube.

The dryer sounds a little bit like people--or at least men. You know how we eat more than we need--and sometimes even more than we want. And then, all things going well, we lose it one way or another. Despite the coming and going of food, people gain weight from this type of activity. Do you suppose that the clothes dryer weighs more than when it was new because of the lint it has retained? If you look into the organs of the dryer, you'll find that the answer is YES.

I'm not sure I like being compared to a clothes dryer.

SERIOUS EXERCISE

You'll recall that I touched on the issue of exercise already. I didn't go into detail on the subject primarily because I'm intimidated by the true fitness buffs. As you know, there are those who are into serious weight lifting, aggressive aerobics and intense cardiovascular workouts. They have muscles out the kadidilhopper. The reason they do and I don't is because my body is stubborn and won't respond to my directives.

Doris told me that she doesn't jog because the action is hard on her knees--but she walks fast. By fast, she means that she walks a six minute mile. A six minute mile!? While I'm brushing, flossing and rinsing, she's walked a mile. She's jogging and just doesn't have the bounce! She walks two miles each morning and two miles each evening. Every day. Granted, she's about twenty years younger than I am, but I decided if she could do it, I could do it, too.

I don't mean I could walk four miles every day; I mean I could walk faster. I can remember a time in my life when I walked a fifteen minute mile instead of my present eighteen minute mile. That was a day or two ago; still, with the right motivation and ambition, I believed I could do it again. I would begin tomorrow.

When tomorrow arrived, my body was less anxious than it was on the yesterday. My brain told me that today wasn't a good day to begin this new routine. Next week would be a fresh week, a new day--so to speak--and, therefore, a much better time to begin an intense exercise program. Obviously, an attitude adjustment session would have to take place, so I began a conversation with myself. The only trouble was that I got flack from the rest of me. Still, there's a time in life when one must lay down the rules regardless of the reason.

With this in mind, I told my bod that the eighteen minute mile that I was presently walking needed to be energized to the point of being a fifteen minute mile--as in the days of yore. I was walking--on the treadmill--at the time of the conversation. The treadmill can be set for speed-- and it will then tell me, joyfully, whether or not I've burned any calories at all. I think it lies because it never wants to admit that I've done anything substantial.

Nonetheless, the treadmill was set for a fifteen minute mile. Some parts of me were not yet ready to work with the mental attitude. Even the shoulders were rebelling, not to mention the hips. I decided to slow the pace to a sixteen minute mile. The objection wasn't much better.

I told my bod that if it would respond for sixteen minutes in the way that I was asking it to, there would be a reward of a candy bar. Then, of course, it would be necessary to walk another sixteen minute mile to burn the calories from the candy bar--but I didn't go into that right then.

The inducement of the candy bar was still insufficient to motivate. Finally, I settled on the eighteen minute mile and tried to hold my head high as I walked from the Fitness Center to our condo. No one else knew about the controversy--and mental defeat--that had just taken place.

Embarrassment at not achieving my goal was not the only sensation that was being felt at this point. There were physical considerations that proved to have more ramifications than the shame. As I struggled to walk upright on the way home, I talked to my parts again.

"What's wrong with you? I tell you to move in certain ways and all you do is resist. Legs, what's gotten into you? I used to tell you to move forward, and you did. I told you to move faster, and you did. Why have you grown so rebellious?

"Shoulders, who asked your opinion? You don't have to do anything except follow the legs. There's no other requirement on you at all; still, you're screaming like a rooster who's just been beheaded.

"Neck, you have your nerve to feel tight and sore. You had less to do than the shoulders which carry you to victory or defeat--so just accept it and get a life!"

By that time, I was home and fell across the bed for a nap.

We'll evaluate the exercise plans next week.

STORIES AND
THE COMPUTER

Have you ever started to tell a story and someone would say, "You told me that before"? Maybe the story is so delicious you really want to tell it again--yet, you're thankful that the person did say that he'd heard it. The computer never does that. I guess it's too polite. You see, when the computer isn't crashing, it really can be a good friend.

You can save something in the computer, turn right around and save it again in the same form with the same name or a different name. If the name is the same, despite the contents, the computer graciously takes the offering. It will tell you that the thing you wish to save already exists, and then ask you if you want to save it anyway--using the same name.

You see, it's this type of graciousness that endears me to the computer--when it isn't kicking me off and making despicable accusations. In addition, it allows me to erase my mistakes without anyone's ever knowing about them--and then it's willing to listen to me tell my story again as I save it. In fact, the computer lets me do this limitless times.

It really is laborious to listen to someone tell the same story several times, with the same minute details and same emphasis on words and points. But the computer doesn't act snippy--except to say that the story already exists in the file and I may want to rename whatever I'm saving at that point.

There are some people who are a bit like this and who rarely talk at all. Maybe they're the listeners, whereas the rest of us are champing at the bit to get our turn to speak.

Some of us have an enormous need for attention? A need to have a better, more complex, worse situation story that the one before--and will even embellish to make the stories such that no one can top them. The computer, on the other hand, sits and listens with just enough response for us to know that it's still tuned in. It never has a one-up-man-ship type of story.

A computer may truly be a person's best friend.

TEENAGE REVISITED

Do you remember the things that were important to you when you were a teenager--for your children or grandchildren? For a male, there's no question that it's (1) girls, (2) car--fast, (3) music--loud, (4) car and (5) girls. The priorities for the girls are (1) boys, (2) boys (3) boys (4) hanging out at the mall and (5) boys. Teenage boys don't ever grow up--or if they do, it's only for a year or two, and then they revert back to that dreaded age. I can't imagine why. My memories are (1) zits, (2) awkwardness, (3) wondering if I'd have a date, and (4) wondering if I'd ever have boobs. But with the masculine gender, I guess there wasn't too much speculation about whether or not he would have boobs, so that was replaced with being the fastest car on the road.

At my present stage in life, I rarely have zits, I don't feel too awkward any more and as a married women, I always have a date as long as I want to do what Hal wants to do. I'm still wondering if I'll ever have boobs. Why would I want to revert to the teenage years?

I do believe, however, that many men do and their focus is a car--fast, weaving in and out, passing the other guy, getting there before anyone else, tailgating and acting silly.

When I met Hal, he was a "mature" man of 24. He didn't drive stupid. In fact, he didn't drive stupid until about 4 or 5 years ago. He was cautious, one who tended to hang back from the crowd of cars and who didn't take chances in passing. Now, he's become a drag racer. If there's a car in front of him, he must overtake it. If there's a truck, he'll race to the end of the highway if necessary. He seems to think that he'll be more successful in his passing strategy if he rides the bumper of the car in front. Now, I, on the other hand. . . .

165

It seems as if my driving habits have changed, also. My usual heavy foot is still heavy, but I tend to hang back from the crowd of cars by several car lengths. I, who previously had a need to lead the pack, am now content to allow someone to be in front of me--and at a discreet distance at that. It seems to me that my driving habits have matured--and represent those of a driver "who has aged gracefully." Whereas Hal represents the person who isn't finished with teenage years. Women of the world, are your men in that same category?   I   t constantly amazes me that Hal gets to and from wherever he's going without being involved in an accident. I think he drives differently when he's alone than when he's with me. When he forgets I'm with him, he's cautious and thoughtful.

Do you think my presence agitates him and he becomes like the rats in the cage that become aggressive from frustration? Or is he still flirting and trying to show off for me?

LISTEN UP AND WRITE IT DOWN

When a woman makes a phone call and is expecting to receive important information, such as directions to the South Pole, ingredients for the recipe for Lamb Flambe or the cost per roll for wallpaper, she has pen and paper in her hand so she can make notes as she listens. Granted it may be the back of an envelope that she's recycling; still, she has tools to record the answers. She may even be seated so she can write better. Seemingly, men don't have those needs. That is, they don't feel the necessity for tools to be able to record important conversations.

If the phone rings and she answers, and if there's a message for the "man of the house," she begins writing immediately to record the message accurately.

A man, on the other hand, calls for the price to demolish the entire condominium. He talks for approximately 30 minutes, asking questions and saying, "I see, oh, it is, already? oh, *not* ready, won't happen, beautiful day, happy New Year to you, too," but he doesn't write a word.

When he gets off the phone, he thinks he's spoken with Mr. Barstow or Carstairs or Rutherford--who said that the air strike was made already but was never intended so there is a retraction to make it not happen, and Mr. whateverhisnameis wished a happy Fourth of July. Those words have no bearing on what the man on your end was repeating, so how can that be the jist of the telephone conversation? Experience tells me that I'll never know what the conversation really was, and there are no notes to make me think otherwise.

When Hal answers the phone on Tuesday and the caller wants to leave a message for Freda, a similar thing happens.

167

On Sunday, Hal asks if he gave me the message that Josephine or Cedrica or some woman with a male sounding name called to say the meeting was on Tuesday--or was it Friday--and I should be prepared to report on native Americans or something like that.

There are no notes, no phone number, I don't know anyone with a name vaguely like the ones he mentioned, and I don't know anything about native Americans or a report that's due. Later when I saw Phyllis, she asked if Hal gave me the message that the committee would meet on Wednesday at the Mirror Lake Library where she would tell us about plans for the art auction.

It reminds me of years ago when our sons took messages. They rarely absorbed any part of it to begin with and they didn't retain it for long--not even to write "Call Sue." Sometimes my messages were important--just as theirs were.

When I answer the phone and take a message, I have two pages of notes. If the writing is less than legible, I go to the computer, type it, laminate the pages, frame them, and hang them on the refrigerator. Ok, I don't frame them.

One day I called our home, Hal answered, and I told him I invited the President of the United States and his wife for dinner tonight. Hal said ok. I asked Hal what he would like to serve for this special family. He said no thought had been given to dinner yet (he's the cook, you know), that he didn't feel very hungry and maybe a grilled cheese sandwich would be fine. I asked Hal if he'd heard a word I'd said. He said he had. I asked him to repeat it. He said I asked him what we were having for dinner tonight.

So, maybe the reason men don't write it down is because they don't hear the conversation in the first place. Bear in mind, this has nothing to do with a hearing loss. Not all men have a hearing loss at 27. This has to do with paying attention and prioritizing things that are important. The way men prioritize is (1) if it's their idea, it's important, (2) if it's their inquiry, it's important, (3) if it's their choice, it's important, (4) if it's their suggestion, it's important (5) if it isn't, it isn't.

Men of the world, grow up. Turn over a new leaf. Will you please pay attention, listen up and write things down!

CHOICES

Women are accustomed to choices. They've always had to decide on color, length, straight or flared, textured or smooth, patterned or solid, dressy or casual, bright or subdued. It didn't matter if it was wall covering, a piece of art, a pair of pants or a washing machine. As difficult as those decisions have been in the past, manufacturers are intent on making them more difficult whether it's clothing, wallpaper or food.

Let's just say that you wanted a pair of jeans. Do you want blue, red, black, khaki, green or white? Oh, you want blue. Do you want periwinkle, faded, stone washed, deep, navy or with barely any color? Do you want a straight leg, a stretch super skinny leg, a generous cut, a flare or a pair you can sit down in? Do you want these to wear to the Little League game, to the office, to the dinner party, to the opera for the Christmas gathering or all of the above?

Do you want the length to fall right at mid calf, slightly above the ankle or below the ankle? Which brand do you want? Lee, Liz, Levi, Gloria or one of a thousand other names?

Is it Lee that's a generous cut, Liz that isn't, Levi or Gloria? You agonize, trying to determine the most versatile pair of jeans for you for all of the purposes for which you want them-- which is all of the above. After all, you may want to wear the jeans to Billy's game in the morning, shop in them in the afternoon, go to the opera in them in the evening and wear them to work on Monday. Jeans don't show soil and don't have to be washed until they're stiff. You don't even have to hang them up at night. The wrinkles seem to disappear the next day--unless they're white, in which case forget all of the above.

People don't seem to remember that you wore jeans yesterday, the day before and the day before that as long as you wear a different top.

You think about the brand with which you've had a good experience in the past. Was it Calvin, Honors, Cherokee, Bill...?

Whichever choice you make, that's the one the store doesn't have. Once your heart is set on having a particular one, that's what you want! Why were you given choices if the style didn't exist in the first place? Ok. You'll take another brand. Oh, that one doesn't exist either. Ok, you'll take a different length. Still no luck. Ok, what *do you have* in a 74 hip size?

Buying wall covering is an equally big decision. You see, if you decide to paint and you don't like it, you just paint over it. Granted, it's a big job to paint the same wall with six different colors before a final decision is made. Have you been there?

There certainly are plenty of colors from which to choose-- in fact, way too many. There are 300 shades of white--not to mention all of the brand choices. It's almost overwhelming.

Wall covering is still another matter. All you have for making a decision is a piece that's about 8" x 8"--that may not even show the true pattern or colors. Then, it has to be ordered, measured, cut, pasted and hung, the store that sold the product isn't too interested in making a refund when you rip it off the walls and return it.

So, it should have come as no great surprise to me today when I decided to make brownies--after five or six years of total abstinence from baking or cooking of any type--and discovered that there were more decisions to be made than I had time or energy for.

Besides the seven brands of brownie mix in this one store, some of which were packaged in a box and some in a plastic bag, I had to decide between (1) double fudge, (2) walnut, (3) dark and fudgy, (4) fudge, (5) double chocolate, (6) peanut butter, (7) original, (8) chocolate chunk, (9) chewy fudge, (10) cheesecake swirl and (11) low fat.

Low fat!!!? A low fat brownie? Really! If you're going to eat a brownie are you concerned about the fat content? Well, maybe so.

Between the brands, the packaging and the types of brownies, there were twenty-seven options from which to choose. As I pondered what to buy, I discovered my bulk was blocking the aisle and had to move it several times to make room for women with carts, babies and handbags that were bigger than our largest suitcase.

I needed to hurry before Hal finished his shopping. No wonder it takes him so long when he goes to the store. How can a person decide between 27 choices for each item needed when each is equally good? This was going to take awhile.

Maybe the decision couldn't be made today. I decided to take a potty break. I couldn't wait until after the decision was made.

LOW FAT, LOW CARBOHYDRATE

When I hear the words "low fat" or "low carbohydrate," I'm skeptical. I know that the product is probably (1) skim milk, (2) broccoli, (3) going to taste awful or (4) something that didn't have any fat to begin with.

Just think about gelatin desserts. There's no fat. Besides that, it's the granddaddy of fast foods. In fact, even a child can make it. Have you ever heard *Jell-O* advertised as low fat or reduced fat? That would be silly. Fat hasn't been reduced in it; there simply never was any fat to begin with.

Skim milk has been around longer than sin. It's almost not fair to advertise skim milk as "low fat." It's true that it has almost no fat in it, but it never did have much fat in it. It always did have all of the other basic ingredients that you would want from milk. So, there's nothing new about *Jell-O* or skim milk.

Hal and I were in a store shopping one day. Armed with wallpaper samples, I was intent on finding just the right towels for our new bathrooms. I was deep in thought, when he tapped me on the shoulder, and in an excited voice, said, "This package says it has no fat. Do you suppose that's true?" If he was holding a towel, I knew the answer was yes. It wasn't a towel.

I took the container, looked at it. It was candy orange slices, covered with about one pound of sugar per slice. I said, "Hal, I believe that's a true statement. There's no fat in those orange slices. On the other hand, there are probably 972 calories in each bite."

You see, the people who talk about fat, don't talk much about carbohydrates or general calories. The people who talk about carbohydrates (carbs), don't usually want to talk about fat or total caloric count. I'm not sure it's fair to prey upon the unsuspecting public (like me) and talk about low carb or the low fat, when you're going to make me look like the Goodyear Blimp from the other calories you've put into the product.

Do you find this type of advertising as confusing and unfair as I do? When you're told that you're eating a low fat whatever, do you ask yourself, "What good is it going to do if I avoid fat but consume more calories from eating a serving than I would if I ate a few fat grams?"

Does it seem to you that the food industry is out to get you? It takes twenty minutes to read the packaging to determine what's in the product. By that time, you have no more energy to check out another brand or a substitute.

I'll tell you what's fair. Show me a food that's low in fat *and* low in carbs. Now, that's the food I need.

Oh, yes, right here it is. It's rice cakes. Oh my, they're really tasty and satisfying. Why don't I just eat the cardboard box in which they're packed and save the rice cakes for company?

THE LENGTH OF THE CANDLE WICK

Where is it written in stone that the length of the candle wick should be one-fourth inch? Who decided that? Was it *Martha Stewart, Heloise* or *Eve*? Regardless of who made the decision, let me tell you my experience.

Everyone knows how a candle wick will smoke if it's too long. I haven't figured out why it does that, but I know it does. In addition, despite the fact that it's stiff as a board from candle wax, it will still curl. Sometimes it curls down, sometimes in an "S" shape and sometimes it just leans like the Tower of Pisa.

Maybe you've tried to do what I have--straighten the wick so the candle will burn nicely and behave itself instead of acting like a recalcitrant child. When the wick is burning in a position other than absolutely upright, the candle doesn't burn properly. That is, it burns more to one side than the other and doesn't have a "perfect" burn hole in the center of the candle. Have you ever had a perfect burn hole?

I use the blade end of a steak knife for the job of straightening the wick, partly because it allows a discrete distance from the burning wick and me and partly because the wood handle of the knife doesn't conduct heat. You see, the procedure has to be done while the wick is pliable--which it wouldn't be if it wasn't hot from burning.

Anyway, I take the blade of the knife and hold the wick straight. While I hold the wick straight, it stays straight. As soon as I remove my tool, the wicked wick goes back to whatever shape it had before--or wants to assume at that particular moment.

Perseverance and time usually triumph. Given enough of both, sprinkled generously with patience, the wick sometimes cleans up its act and becomes upright.

Now, on the other hand, if the wick is shortened to one-fourth inch, a process to which I've tried to be faithful, it's sometimes angered. It could be likened to a woman who has her long hair cut short. It's a shock.

You see, the shortness of the wick limits the number of curves and curls that it can make--and sometimes the end result is that the wick won't burn at all. I've experienced this with a new candle, a slightly burned one and a grossly burned. There's a very fine line insofar as length is concerned, when one is dealing with the wick and temperament of a candle.

In addition to all of this information that you've undoubtedly found enormously informative, not all wicks burn at the same degree of speed. I'm assuming the speed has to do with the wick and the wax. Sometimes, the wick becomes too long shortly after beginning to burn and it smokes. That's another story. Suffice it to say that it's better if a wick doesn't burn at all than to smoke.

On one particular occasion I had set up a special display of candles. Really, if I do say so myself, it was glorious. It was for the Fourth of July. There was a pleasing, royal blue candle that was eight inches tall and four inches in diameter, two smaller red candles that weren't Christmas red--and some white candles, all of different heights.

The final wonderful thing was the package of thin stones in shades of blue. These were scattered around the candles that were placed on a large, clear crystal serving platter. There were seven candles, surrounded by the stones--and several frogs.

I trimmed the wicks before lighting them. They were of uniform length, and I was set for a most proper burn of the candles so they could be used again and again, not only during this season but in future seasons as well. Of course, I don't know where I thought the candles would be stored until the next Fourth of July.

Imagine my surprise when one of the white pillar candles-- the nine inch one--wouldn't respond to the match that was held at the top of the wick. I began to pry out some of the wax around it. The wick still didn't recognize my efforts. More wax was removed. The wax and the wick simply would not cooperate. I gave up that evening, but on the morrow (I just love that expression, don't you?), I decided I would light that puppy whether or not it was a willing participant.

So, back to my original question, who decided that a one-fourth inch wick was the be all and end all of good candle burning?

THE HONOR OF BEING NUMBER ONE

Do you know how the dentists label your teeth? Did you think it was by "the big front tooth on the left" or "incisor on the top right" or "twelve year molar"? Well, that isn't the way at all. The dentist simply counts. In educating you about the procedure, may I refer to the dentist as a he and may I tell you that number one isn't where you would think?

He begins counting on the upper right, works his way over to the left (that's your body, not his) and then goes below from the left to the right. That means that the number one tooth is the Wisdom Tooth on the upper right, which most people have had removed--assuming they, unlike me, ever had one at all. You see, I have no Wisdom Teeth. Never did. Perhaps that accounts for many things. I figured that I might as well say it before you did.

Have you ever wondered why a "Wisdom Tooth" is called by that name?

The Second Year Molars come in when a child is about two years old. The Six Year Molars and the Twelve Year Molars, on average, also are "cut" at about the mentioned age. The Wisdom Teeth, however, are more apt to come in during the teenage years. I hardly think that age could be considered one of wisdom.

Let's get on with the counting process. When you consider that almost no one has a Number One tooth because it has been removed or never came through the gum in the first place, that same person very possibly doesn't have a number fifteen tooth, a number sixteen or a number thirty-two. Personally, I don't care much about the number fifteen, sixteen or thirty-two. However, I do care about the number one.

Anyone who has ever been "Number One" knows the thrill of it. Well, I guess a person would be thrilled; I haven't experienced it yet. Were you ever thrilled to be number twenty-nine? I don't think so.

Now, take my mouth. Ok, smartie, so you don't want my mouth--who would? In my mouth, there is no "Number One" tooth. As I've already told you, that would be a wisdom tooth, upper, on the right side. I don't have one. Never did. Yes, I've felt short-changed and it has impacted my personality and drive considerably. There's no telling what I could have done with my life if I had possessed a Number One tooth--even though I didn't know it was the Number One tooth until a month or two ago when I heard the dentist counting my teeth and making comments about them to his assistant.

Don't tell me all persons are created equally. How could you possibly say that when I never had a Number One tooth and you did? It was your choice to have it removed, you know. Until this moment, the shame of lacking a Number One tooth has caused me to keep this information safely locked within my head--even though I was totally unaware of it until just a short time ago.

Only my former dentist knew about the lack of a Number One tooth in my mouth, and he was discrete enough not to reveal this even to me. My question is, did the honor of being the number one tooth go by default to the next tooth--which some of us commonly know as the "Twelve Year Molar"? No. No, the honor didn't go anywhere. It just died. It was wasted.

Now, on the other hand, had the dentists chosen to begin counting at, say, the upper center tooth (the big, broad one) on the right, the Number One position would rarely have been wasted. Even if the tooth had decay--which it doesn't nearly as often as the molars--it would still have the honor. Even if the tooth had been covered to make it more attractive in the eyes of the person proposing the capping, it would still be there-- even though it had been altered. Even if the tooth had to be

182

removed, a bridge or a denture of some sort would likely have replaced it. So, there would always be a Number One tooth.

To be fair, the big center, upper tooth (the broad one again) to the left could have been the Number One tooth after a person reached the age of, say, twenty-five. Then the numbering system could have proceeded from center to left instead of center to right.

When a person became fifty--the highlight of everyone's life--the bottom, center, right tooth could become Number One and the numbering system continue from center to right on the lower part of the mouth. Then at age seventy-five, the direction could change from center to left.

Even this system has flaws, of course, because some people don't live much beyond seventy-five--if they reach that mark at all. For that matter, some don't reach fifty. And, of course, some don't make it to twenty-five. Still, it would have shown a good faith effort at equality for the mouth. And the owner of the mouth.

Anyway, under the best of circumstances, that system would provide the opportunity for four different teeth to be in the Number One position. Granted, it still wouldn't be fair--and would be discriminatory--for all but these four teeth. Still, surely it would provide more equality than the present system.

Another suitable counting system would be to use the alphabet. I can see and hear it now. The dentist would say to his assistant, "Teeth A and P are missing, tooth C needs a crown, tooth D isn't long for this world." Even a preschooler could make a song of it using the melody of the ABC Song. It would go like this

X and Y were pulled last week,
H and I went by-by in my sleep.
U and Z soon will leap
J and G now must peep
Look, I've lost all my front teeth.

Now, granted, there's a small problem with using the alphabet. In the first place, there aren't enough letters. However, by using double A, double B and so on, the system would work.

All I'm saying is that the alphabet would reduce the possibility of hurt feelings because there was no possible chance of ever having, or being, the Number One tooth.

You may not take this subject as seriously as I do. Number One has evaded me for years. No matter what I did, there was always someone else ready to step up to the plate to take the Number One honor. That person may not have had as many overall attributes as I (how could anyone?) but the person still won the honor at the moment of being Number One.

As best I can remember, I was not the first person born on this earth. Not even in my family. I have never been the first member of any group. I was not the Number One best speller. I certainly was not the Number One most beautiful in my class, or the Number One person voted by my high school peers as the most likely to succeed or the person with the Number One best personality.

If I had a Number One tooth, that knowledge in itself might have made a difference in my life. I might have been the first woman astronaut--or the first woman President of the United States.

THE EARLY BIRDS

You know all about the early bird getting the worm and how much you can get done before the rest of the world gets started--if you get up early. But just think about those statements, dissect them and ask yourself if early rising may be mistake.

Hal and I get up early. On one particular morning, by 7:00, we were dressed, had finished breakfast, brushed, flossed and rinsed and had checked for email. I unloaded the dishwasher, and that was when it happened. In the process of putting some things away and cleaning off the stove, I looked up. Oh, what a mistake!

There were two screws holding a part of the microwave. These screws had been noted before. However, this was the first time I paused long enough to get a Phillips head screwdriver to take the piece off.

It was necessary to stand on the step stool to do it. Oh, woe is me--what I saw while standing there! Grease was on the top front of the cabinets and had made running paths--right in plain view. Well, plain view for me because I was on a step stool.

The grease was high enough not to be seen under normal conditions. However, now that I was in an abnormal condition--position on the step stool and had seen the grease, what was I to do? Besides that, there was food--or something--on the ceiling. You've heard that what goes up must come down? Well, don't put too much faith in that, because whatever went "up" to the ceiling, was still there.

What prompted all of this? Removing the part on the microwave I mean. We were having company. When we have company we start with the closets and disinfect everything.

Well, I didn't start with the closets this time. In fact, I didn't start with anything. I was taking the position--which I always do until twenty-four hours before blast off--that things were all right just as they were.

Still, somehow the grease was sufficient to demand cleaning the high cabinets and the ceiling of the kitchen--and that led to cleaning the rails of the deck.

I don't know how the kitchen led to the rails of the deck. It just did. And they were dirty! The rails--of the deck. Just suppose that this cleaning--both inside and outside--had been overlooked. Just suppose our children had arrived and had seen the dirt on the top cabinets--which is well above eye level. Just suppose our children had leaned against the rails of the deck--or had *touched* the rails and had felt the dirt!

Unfortunately, while still on the deck, I turned around and looked at our chairs and table. Granted, they were just fine for Hal and me and some of our friends to sit in, despite the dirt, and we hadn't ruined any of our clothes by sitting on them--so far. But they were dirty. In the first place the chairs are white with white mesh seats and back. White, just like the rails of the deck.

It took a lot of cleaner and elbow grease to clean the four chairs, the table and the rails. You know, there's more to a chair than just the arms and the seat. There's all of the supporting structure underneath. For the table, too.

There was no question that our children were going to get down on their hands and knees to look at the supporting structure to determine if there was any dirt there--just as I did to discover it in the first place. And they'll also probably get the step stool and look at the tops of the cabinets and the ceiling of the kitchen.

It would be a pity if you were to think that we clean everything every week--when actually we only do a few things once in a while--and not until it's an absolute necessity such as the failure of an appliance to function because of dirt and grime. The microwave exhaust hadn't failed to function--yet. Based on the appearance of things, however, it was only a matter of seconds--or years.

This was an excellent day to begin the mentioned projects because I had an appointment with the dentist to have a crown installed, Hal had an appointment to have the "air bag" serviced (puhleeze, before you even think it, I mean the air bag in the car). So, of course, one would want to begin a major cleaning project on a day when time-consuming errands were also planned.

The next time we have company, we're going to take sheets and drape the deck rails, the deck chairs, the microwave and the cabinet above it. And the floor ... .